The Peace and I

2020 The Forgotten Leap Year

Part 2

By

Vendon Wright

Shield Crest

© Copyright 2023 Vendon Wright

All rights reserved.

ISBN: 978-1-915657-31-2

MMXXIII

A CIP catalogue record for this book
is available from the British Library.

Published by
ShieldCrest Publishing,
Boston, Lincolnshire,
PE20 3BT England
Tel: +44 (0) 333 8000 890

www.shieldcrest.co.uk

Acknowledgements

Inspired by - Tanya Grant Davis

Editor – Flossie Crossie.

Devoted to - In loving memory of my
dear sister Alirthe Wright and brother Leroy
Wright, who both passed away in January
2020

Chapter 1

Violet's world seemed quieter than the one they had left behind. Lexie and her Rainbow sister, Violet had emerged from their portal four hundred years into the future and were about to receive a surprise welcome.

"It almost appears to be deserted," commented Lexie whilst observing her surroundings.

"Yes, it does," returned Violet hesitantly.

The world Violet had left behind was thriving with people, with almost overpopulated countries. Their main worry was Dr Dre, a mad Scientist that was trying to destroy the world with advanced nuclear weaponry. Now that Violet had returned to the future, either people were hiding or there was a definite shortage.

"Are you sure we have arrived at the correct time in the future?"

"My GPS on my mobile says we are home, so one of these houses should be mine."

"What? Don't you even recognise your own house?"

"No, everything looks slightly different."

They slowly walked towards the house. It was a three-story house that looked like it was made from plastic.

"What, do you live in a doll's house?" Lexie asked curiously.

Violet chuckled and then said, "No, silly, it's made out of reinforced plastic."

"That's what I said," repeated Lexie, "a doll's house."

"Houses these days are made from metallic plastic to super absorb the sun's rays. They are stronger than concrete. The insulated plastic around the house itself stores the solar energy to heat and fuel the home. Now the whole house is a solar panel."

"I bet your gas bills are cheap."

"We stopped using conventional gas over three hundred years ago."

"Why?"

"To keep down the level of methane gas building up in the atmosphere."

"What about petrol and diesel?"

"We stopped using them over three hundred years ago too."

"So, everything is electric based?"

"Electric and electromagnetic," answered Violet.

Just then Lexie sensed something that was beginning to irritate her eardrum. It was a buzzing sound progressively getting louder.

"What's that annoying noise?"

"I don't hear anything," answered Violet.

A few seconds later she too heard the buzzing and said, "How were you able to hear that before me?"

"I guess my hearing has become more sensitive."

"So you have developed canine senses like a dog??"

Lexie chuckled.

Seconds later, the police turned up. They were in futuristic vehicles called Hover-cars. The noise they made was like a giant swarm of bees, easy to hear and annoying enough to attract everyone's attention. They swooped in and slowly glided to the ground. Two Officers appeared out of a Hover-car with two dogs, two big dogs growling furiously towards the girls. Several Officers appeared out of another hover-car with weapons similar to that of Dr Dre's Proton gun, pointing towards the girls.

"LAPD, Freeze," one of the Officers ordered.

"What should we do?" asked Lexie.

"Don't move," replied Violet, "unless you want to be eaten by those big dogs."

"They are not dogs," whispered Lexie, "they are more like a horse."

"How did they know of our arrival?" muttered Violet softly.

"Maybe the other Rainbow girls mentioned it," replied Lexie.

"No, somethings not quite right," responded Violet.

A commanding Officer began to shout orders.

"Put your hands up so that we can see them clearly."

The girls put their hands high into the air and stared towards the huge dogs.

"Maybe we should go into telepathy mode," suggested Lexie.

The girls remained silent as one of the Officers approached.

"Have you noticed that they are all wearing sunglasses?" commented Violet telepathically.

"Well, it is very hot, maybe too hot for March," replied Lexie who was now using her new telepathic abilities.

"No, they know who we are and have come out prepared, shields up."

"What are you two girls doing in this neighbourhood without permission?"

"I live here," replied Violet.

"Where's your neighbourhood pass?" he asked.

"Err, I must have left it in my house."

"And you?" he directed towards Lexie.

"Say you are a friend visiting from out of town," suggested Violet.

"I'm a friend visiting from out of town," answered Lexie.

"Where's your electronic proof of identity?" he asked in a commanding tone.

The dogs began to snarl, growling ferociously towards them.

"We left everything in the house," answered Lexie.

"Sorry, but we have to follow rules and arrest you, just in case you are planning to take part in a criminal activity."

"Wait; what?" said Violet, "my parents are in the house, just ask them and they will tell you I am their daughter."

Two more Officers approached and quickly placed handcuffs firmly around their wrists.

"Don't resist," advised Violet using telekinesis.

Both girls remained silent.

The commanding Officer approached Violet and placed his arm on her shoulder. He then radios a message to someone on his phone. Lexie listened in and was surprised to be able to hear the person on the other end clearly.

"Could you hear the person on the other end of the phone?" asked Lexie.

"No, why could you?" asked Violet.

"Yes."

"What did they say?"

"They asked if they managed to apprehend the two girls that appeared out of the portal."

"They know who we are."

"How?"

"I don't know so be on your guard for anything."

The girls continued their conversation telepathically without any of the police officers knowing.

"What else did the other person say?" asked Violet.

"He said not to take their eyes off us and to wait while he sends a helicopter to pick us up and bring us in for questioning."

"Then prepare yourself for trouble," advised Violet.

"I've got some more bad news," Lexie announced.

"What?"

"I think that I recognised the other person's voice."

"Who did they sound like?"

"Dr Dre."

Violet's eyes widened as the sound of a helicopter became louder. It slowly glided down to the ground before Lexie realised that the helicopter had no rotary blades.

"How is it flying without rotating blades?"

"Technology has moved forwards in the last few hundred years."

Two Officers led the girls to the helicopter and assisted them inside. The helicopter lifted smoothly and glided off.

They landed in the courtyard of the LAPD Station and were then led into an interrogation room. An Officer sat before them and began his questioning.

"Name, address and contact details," he asked.

Violet was able to answer but Lexie hesitated while waiting for some assistance.

"Say you live with me," suggested Violet telepathically.

The Officer noted it all on his electro-base on his mobile phone, a replacement for conventional computers. He then looked up and said, "I thought you said you were visiting from out of town?"

"I was, I mean I did, but now I am staying with family," replied Lexie.

Unbeknown to the Officer, Violet was relaying messages to Lexie using telekinesis.

"Parent's name and contact details?" he asked.

Lexie waited for more suggestions from Violet.

"My mum's name is Wendy, and my dad is called Francisco," replied Lexie.

"Wait just a minute," said the Officer abruptly, "that's the same as Violet's parents."

"We are sisters, stepsisters," Lexie stuttered.

"And your mother?" he asked.

"We are all mothers."

"What?" said the Officer sounding slightly alarmed.

"My mother is her mother, we all have the same mother," Lexie corrected.

The Officer rolled his eyes and looked baffled.

He then asked Violet for her age and date of birth.

"I am fourteen and my date of birth is 5th June 2405."

"That makes you fifteen," the Officer corrected.

"Err, can't you count?" Violet asked sarcastically.

He ignored her comment and directed the same questions towards Lexie.

She hesitated while saying,

"Err, I'm twelve and my date of birth is, my date of birth is 5th June 2407, wait, that makes us twins."

Violet smiled.

"That makes you thirteen," the Officer corrected.

"You told me the wrong date," complained Lexie telepathically.

"I'm sure that's correct," replied Violet.

"Are you girls going to start telling me the correct information or do I have to call for some assistance?"

"We are Sir," answered Lexie.

"Out of curiosity, what is today's date?" asked Violet.

"It's Sunday 26 July 2420," he answered.

Violet gazed towards Lexie and then turned back to face the officer.

"That's impossible," Violet commented, "where has nearly five months of our lives gone?"

"Are you saying I missed my 13th Birthday?" asked Lexie disappointingly.

The officer stared into her emerald green eyes.

"I missed my 15th Birthday too," said Violet.

The Officer turned his head to look directly into Violet's big blue eyes, gave her a blank stare and then said,

"I've had enough of being messed around! I'm going to call your parents."

With that, he swiftly left the room.

Lexie quickly turned to Violet and said, "What's going on?"

"Something's wrong," replied Violet, "we should have emerged from the portal at the end of March."

Violet consulted her mobile and then went silent.

"Something wrong?" asked Lexie.

"My mobile now says it's July, how is that possible?"

"Someone's messing with time," answered Lexie.

"But... but how could the balance of time be altered?" stuttered Violet.

"I'm telling you" answered Lexie, "Dr Dre is back."

Chapter 2

The girls stared towards each other for a second or two. Then Violet broke the silence and whispered, "You destroyed Dr Dre, you blew him up, he's gone."

"Not gone forever though," replied Lexie.

"What are you implying?"

"Dr Dre was immortal."

"Immortal means that you live forever, but it doesn't mean you can't die."

"What does that even mean?"

"Stop worrying, he's vanished, gone," advised Violet.

"Then who's voice did I hear on the phone?"

"I'm telling you, Dr Dre's voice is just a figment of your imagination."

"Then who's messing with time?"

"Maybe the universe is still trying to find a balance."

"Well, it better hurry, or hypothetically speaking, we are screwed," warned Lexie.

"Don't be so melodramatic," replied Violet.

"We need to find the vaccine and then I will use the portal to get back and save everyone in my world."

There was more silence, while Violet ran through some scenarios in her mind before drawing to a conclusion.

"We need to get out of here."

"How are we going to avert the police?"

"Who cares about them, let's fly out of here in an instant."

"What's that noise?" Lexie asked as she slowly looked around to identify its whereabouts.

"I hear nothing," replied Violet.

There was a gentle buzzing noise.

"It's getting louder, can't you hear it?" asked Lexie.

"Yes, I hear it now, that doesn't sound good, come on, let's get out of here," returned Violet.

Both girls broke-out of their handcuffs as though they were weak strands of string and prepared to fly off, but there was no movement.

"What's going on?" asked Lexie.

"I'm grounded and can't fly," answered Violet.

"Maybe that noise is some type of electro-magnetic force preventing us from leaving."

"We are trapped," concluded Violet.

The outer level of the walls began to rise to reveal several guns hidden behind, which were all now pointing towards them. There was also a CCTV camera that sounded like it was zooming in.

"Any last-minute ideas?" asked Lexie, growing nervous.

"What special powers are you packing these days?" asked Violet.

"I think that we are about to find out," answered Lexie.

The guns began to fire rapid bullets towards them both. Their shields were up causing the bullets to bounce off them like ping pong balls, leaving them unharmed. After a few seconds the sound of gun fire grew silent.

"Is that it?" asked Violet.

"I don't think so," replied Lexie.

There was an even louder buzzing sound. Suddenly red, white and blue laser beams were seen. The colourful crystal gemstones on their belts lit up, increasing the power of their invisible force field to withstand the energy from the proton guns. After a few more seconds, the gun fire stopped. There was silence while both girls quickly glanced around the room.

"Is it all over?" asked Violet.

"I think that they are testing us to see what superpowers we have," said Lexie, "so I sense that there is more to come."

A small hole appeared in one of the walls.

"Okay," said Violet calmly.

Several hand grenades began to fly out of the hole and bounce across the floor.

"Not okay," squealed Lexie.

There were about twelve hand grenades that lay silent. Then, there was an almighty explosion that echoed all around the room. When the smoke disappeared, the two girls were clearly seen, still very much alive.

"Is that all you've got?" Violet shouted.

"That blast messed up my hair," said Lexie, fixing her hair band straight.

There was silence for a few seconds, but then Lexie sensed something else.

"I think that they are about to electrify the floor."

"We'll get fried, we can't fly," said Violet, sounding unsure.

"I believe I can fly," said Lexie.

"No time for a song," commented Violet, "holy moly, what are we going to do?"

Lexie held firmly onto Violet's hand and said,

"Run."

They began to run just as the ground became electrified. Lexie was running so fast with Violet held firmly in her grasp, that the current omitted from the pressure sensors did not have time to electrocute them. The people observing the effects from the CCTV could only see a colourful blur whizzing around and around the room at high velocity. Lexie continued to run at high speed with Violet hanging on for her dear life.

"What the hell!" screamed Violet.

"Who's melodramatic now?" responded Lexie telepathically.

After about ten seconds the loud buzzing sound dissipated. Lexie sensed that the floor was no longer electrified, so reduced her speed and slowly came to a stop. The two teenage girls stood there in perfect view, clearly unharmed. Suddenly the ground began to move as though it wanted to rotate. Lexie's amber crystal on her belt began to flash and they both hovered just above the floor. When the floor finally finished rotating upside down, it revealed a formation of furniture similar to that which had been destroyed with all the gunfire.

"Do you think that they have finished testing us now?" asked Violet.

"Yes," answered Lexie.

"Your powers are advancing," encouraged Violet.

"I know, right!" replied Lexie joyfully.

The door opened and the same police officer entered the room.

"How are you?" he asked plainly.

"Amazing," replied Lexie sarcastically.

"Why are you girls standing up?" he asked innocently.

"You've just tried to kill us," said Lexie.

"What?" he responded, "I wasn't even in the room."

"There were guns firing at us from the walls," said Violet.

He glanced towards all the walls and then said,

"There is no sign of guns anywhere."

The girls rotated on their heels and had a detailed look at the walls. They noticed that the outer layer of the walls had covered all the guns to leave a smooth shiny finish.

"I saw guns and they fired bullets at us," said Violet.

"Did they hit you?" he asked.

"No, they missed," replied Lexie cleverly.

He surveyed the room again and said,

"Then where's the bullets?"

"They must have disappeared," said Violet.

"I think you girls are inventing stories."

"You were testing to see what special abilities we had," said Lexie.

"Have you got special powers?" he asked as he gave a slight disbelieving chuckle.

"You are not experimenting on us anymore," said Violet sternly, "we are leaving."

"I have to search you first, to see if you are concealing any weapons."

"You are not touching us," Lexie insisted boldly.

"Please remove your belts from around your waist," he ordered.

"That's illegal," said Violet, "we are underage."

"We demand a phone call to contact our parents," added Lexie.

"No need," he answered, "your mum is already waiting in the reception area for you."

"Then I demand to see my mum, now!" responded Violet with fury.

The Officer sighed deeply and then hastily left the room.

As he left, Lexie quickly turned to face Violet and said,

"Oh wow, I get to meet your mum."

"You might get a little bit of a surprise," replied Violet.

"Why?"

Just then the door opened and the officer entered with a beautiful young lady standing by his side.

"What have they done to you, my pet?" she asked, directing her speech towards Violet.

"Hi mum."

Lexie stood there, staring at Violet's mum. It felt as though she was staring into a mirror, for Violet's mum looked identical to Lexie. She had black wavy hair down to her shoulders and emerald-green eyes and was now looking directly towards Lexie.

"And who is this gorgeous girl with you?"

"This is Lexie."

"I thought that you were sisters?" asked the officer in confusion.

"Can't you see the uncanny resemblance to me?" said Violet's mum.

"Hi mum," said Lexie with a bright smile.

The Officer shook his head puzzled with the strange reunion.

"Hi, my child," she answered, "my name is Wendy, Violet's mum."

"Mum," said Lexie with a slight chuckle, "I know your name,"

"Mum, you are so funny," interjected Violet, "imagine forgetting your other daughter's name."

"Well, it's been a long time since I last saw her."

The three girls giggled together, while the Officer became even more baffled.

A few seconds later, the Officer turned to face their mum and said, "Please could I have consent to search your daughters?"

Their mum turned and stared towards the girls. When Wendy was staring directly into Violet's big blue eyes, she blinked. Wendy was now under mind control and Violet compelled her to agree with their proposals.

"Please mum, don't allow him to touch us."

"Could you ask them to remove their belts?" the Officer asked.

"Say no mum," Lexie pleaded.

Wendy seamed to pause with thought and then said, "No, I want to take my two daughters home right now."

Both girls smiled triumphantly. The Officer hastily agreed, but then said, "You will both have to come back in tomorrow morning to be tagged."

"What does he mean tagged, mum?" Violet asked.

"Everyone has to be tagged now."

"Why?"

"So that the authorities can track everyone to minimise criminal activities."

"We are not criminals," said Lexie in a slight huff.

"Everyone is tagged, including your mum," interjected the Officer.

"Are you mum?" Violet asked in a raised tone.

"Yes."

Just then Violet's mum turned her head to one side and gently brushed her hair back away from her right ear to reveal a small mark.

"Whatever is that?" asked Lexie, becoming deeply concerned.

"It is a small barcode that all thirteen year olds and above have stamped on their head," said the Officer.

"Is it the mark of the beast?" asked Violet.

"No my Pet," said Wendy, "it's a digital tracker, it's safe and painless, everyone wears one now."

"We can't have that done to us," Violet insisted emphatically.

"Why not?" asked the Officer.

"We have to be somewhere important," answered Violet.

"Where?" asked Wendy.

Lexie's head swam with thought for a moment, then she said,

"Don't we have to be at school in the morning?"

The Officer glanced at Wendy and said,

"I want them back here straight after school finishes tomorrow."

Wendy paused, glanced at Violet's blue eyes and then quickly agreed.

On the way out, Lexie and Violet spoke to each other telepathically.

"We can't be tracked," said Lexie, "we can't have anyone knowing what we are doing."

"I know," replied Violet, "we have a few more hours to find your vaccine and then get you back to your world."

"Yes," said Lexie, "that's priority now."

"The faster you go back through the portal, the quicker you can return everything back to normal."

Chapter 3

O utside the Police station was a huge shiny, metallic Hover-car.

"Cool, who's ride is this?" asked Lexie in excitement.

"Mine," replied Wendy with a proud smile.

"It's a bit bigger than I remember," said Violet as they climbed aboard and strapped themselves in.

"What a magnificent piece of equipment," admired Lexie.

Wendy pressed a few buttons and they slowly glided off. It had a stick instead of a steering wheel and smelled so new. All the controls were on the front window. It was like looking at a computer monitor with several smaller screens on the right and left arranged vertically.

"How fast can this baby go?" Lexie asked excitedly.

"Hover-cars go a little faster than your conventional cars, but we are still limited to certain speeds," answered Wendy.

"Everything is computerised so as to minimise accidents," said Violet.

"Watch this," said Wendy as she accelerated.

Within seconds she was behind another hover-car.

"I am still accelerating," boasted Wendy proudly, "but as you can clearly see, we are not getting any closer to the vehicle in front. That's because the computer on board has taken over and is now in control."

The floor of the hover-car began to vibrate violently, giving Lexie a surprise, but Wendy and Violet giggled cheerfully.

"What was that?" asked Lexie enquiringly.

"Don't worry," smiled Wendy, "that was also the computer purposefully shaking us, just in case we had accidently fallen asleep at the controls."

They all giggled joyfully and in just a short moment they were setting down, back in front of Violet's house.

On the way to the front door, Violet turned her head to look over her shoulder at the park nearby.

"The park is empty, where is everyone?"

"Towns are no longer overcrowded."

"That park is normally overflowing with parents and their children, so where has everyone gone?"

"People started disappearing several months ago," replied Wendy.

"Around the end of March?" asked Lexie.

Wendy turned to face her and said, "Yes."

The girls fell silent, so Wendy turned back around and entered the house. During that short moment, both girls returned into telepathy mode.

"We have affected everything with our presence," said Violet.

"We need to find that vaccine fast and get me back home," insisted Lexie.

"Time here has definitely been altered."

"Now that four months are missing, I wonder what kind of world I have to go back to?"

"Maybe your time has also been affected."

"Our primary mission is to retrieve the vaccine and return me back home."

"Okay, nothing can stand in our way."

"Do you know where to start searching?"

"The UCLA university has a cutting-edge science department, which has developed hundreds of vaccines for destroying viruses. It is the best in the Country."

"That's the same University we visited in my time."

"Well, let's hope there are no surprises waiting for us," responded Violet.

They closed the door behind them.

"Welcome to our humble home," said Wendy.

Violet glanced around and was overjoyed to see her dog.

"Orion," she called, "I'm home, come to mamma."

The dog slowly raised his head, had a quick glance towards Violet and then placed his head back on the floor lazily.

"What's happened to Orion?" asked Violet, becoming concerned.

"He has missed you," replied Wendy.

"He's normally much more lively to see me."

"You've been gone for several months."

"I thought that I would get a warmer welcome than that. Mamma's feeling sad now."

"I've got some more sad news," said Wendy in a soft tone.

"What?" said Violet nervously.

"Your father has been sectioned."

"Wait, what?"

"He couldn't cope with your disappearance and had a psychotic break."

"I am so sorry to hear that," said Lexie.

"What do you mean he had a psychotic break?" screamed Violet.

"He thought that you were dead, murdered or even worse."

"So it's my fault?"

Wendy paused for a second and then said,

"Sit down, both of you, let me go and make you a cup of Tea, or even something stronger."

"Say what now?" said Lexie.

"Would you like to join us in drinking this Authentic Russian Rum?"

"I thought Russians liked to drink Vodka?" questioned Lexie.

"I assure you; this is much more potent."

"You do know that we are only teenagers?"

"Have a drink," Wendy insisted.

"No thanks, I think that I will stick to the Tea," concluded Lexie.

Violet remained silent, still surprised with the news of her father.

Lexie glared at the dog and noticed it didn't look healthy.

"That dog doesn't look well."

"It's probably my fault," answered Violet, "maybe it has refused to eat for months."

"What made you call him Orion?"

"He immediately took a liking to my magical belt."

"Why does your mum keep calling you Pet?"

"When I was small, I would sometimes go missing and my mum would find me sleeping on the dog's bed."

Lexie chuckled just as Wendy entered the room with their cups of Tea. She handed them their cups with a few biscuits.

"There you go my Pet and here's yours, Lexie."

They took a sip of their tea.

"So, where are you from, Lexie?" Wendy asked.

"I'm from the past."

"How is that possible?"

"It's a bit confusing to explain, but I am here to find an antidote for my world."

"You think that we have a vaccine here?"

Lexie glanced towards Violet for some assistance, but she sipped on her tea in silence.

"Yes," continued Lexie, "we are now connected to the future through a portal, and we travelled here to retrieve the vaccine and return it as soon as possible."

"So that's where you were for the last few months Pet?"

Violet was still in shock so remained quiet.

"Your daughter has amazing abilities," said Lexie.

"How is it that you look like a spitting image of me?" asked Wendy.

"I guess we are all related," said Lexie.

"Then I guess I really am your mum then," Wendy chuckled.

"I'm from the past, so that makes me your mum or grandma or something," Lexie sniggered.

"Yes, I suppose you are right... grandma," replied Wendy.

They both giggled joyfully.

There was silence for a few seconds while they both waited for Violet to join in with the conversation, but there was no response. Violet just sat there sipping away at her tea, so Lexie helped herself to some biscuits.

"So, it's clear that I got my good looks from your side of the family," said Wendy.

"Of course," boasted Lexie, "but who did I even get with to have, well, children?"

"I don't know," replied Wendy, "but My husband says he carries his family name from his Mexican ancestry. He immigrated to Dominica, which is where Violet was born and then we settled in America."

"Are you saying that I have ancestors in Mexico?"

"Yes, of course."

"What did you say your husband's name is?" Lexie asked hesitantly.

"Francisco."

Lexie began to giggle again. She then turned towards Violet saying,

"I thought that Francisco fancied you?"

"I guess he went after me because he wanted to make you jealous," said Violet in a serious voice.

"So, Francisco is your dad," said Lexie without knowing that Violet would revert back to thinking about her immediate father.

Totally ignoring Lexie, Violet took a few more sips from her tea, turned to face her mum and then said,

"Where are they keeping dad?"

"In the hospital next to the Police Station," answered Wendy.

"I need to visit him."

"He's not in a fit state to receive visitors."

"Why, has he gone crazy?"

"He has had a psychological breakdown."

Lexie took a sip of her tea and kept out of the conversation.

"Dad was the most positive person I know," said Violet, "he would be the last person that would have depression or a nervous breakdown, no, no, something else must have caused him to lose it."

"It could happen to anyone," said Wendy, "it doesn't matter how strong you are, all it takes is something to push you over the edge."

"So, my absence pushed him over the edge?" asked Violet, now becoming tearful.

"The stress of thinking that he lost you was too much for him to bear."

Lexie turned her head towards Violet and became worried, because that was the first time she had seen her express any real emotions. Violet would be the one that normally told others to control their emotions and here she was, crying, with real tears falling from her eyes. Lexie sensed that something wasn't quite right.

"I'm sorry Pet, it could happen to the best of us, it could even happen to you or I if we are overloaded with information, our brains can only take a certain amount of information before it shuts down."

"I use 70% of my brain, how could it ever happen to me?"

"It could happen to both of you," replied Wendy who now turned her head to face Lexie, "all humans are prone to stress, anxiety and depression, all it takes is a gentle push."

"That's why I limit negative input," said Lexie.

"So, you don't want to know about my father?" asked Violet in a raised tone.

"Yes but-"

"You are only interested in finding a vaccine and returning to your world," interrupted Violet.

"No, no, that's not true," defended Lexie.

Wendy remained silent and observed the girls.

"You don't care about me anymore," said Violet.

"I love you like a sister," said Lexie.

"You only love people from your world."

"What's happened to you?" Lexie asked, "this isn't like you."

Violet put her head into both her hands and screamed,

"Why is this happening to me? I can't take anymore."

Lexie glanced towards Wendy for some assistance.

"Do you know what's happening to Violet?"

"When it rains, it pours," replied Wendy.

"I don't understand?" returned Lexie, now growing concerned for Violet's mental health.

"She has too many issues to deal with," answered Wendy, "we all have a tolerance level, a point that we can't go on and we become overwhelmed with information. Violet is a strong mountain, but if you bombarded a mountain enough times with water, it soon begins to crack."

"Are you saying Violet has an information overload and is cracking up?"

"Yes, I think that she needs psychological help."

"I've just been trying to get help from my Rainbow girls, but nobody is answering their mobiles," interjected Violet.

"What, nobody?" asked Lexie.

"No, I tried Red, India, Gloria, Helen and Tamir, but nobody's responding."

There was a slight pause, then her mum said,

"I'm afraid I have even more sad news."

"I have reached my limit and I really can't take anymore sad news," said Violet.

"What is it?" asked Lexie.

"Roxie Red has had an accident."

"Is she alright?" asked Violet who suddenly became deeply concerned.

"She died," answered Wendy.

The girls suddenly sat bolt upright in their seats. Then Violet yelled,

"But she's supposed to be immortal."

Chapter 4

"So, what happened to Red?" Lexie asked with deep sympathy.

"Apparently she went Skiing and hit a tree," replied Wendy.

"Surely that wouldn't harm her," remarked Lexie.

"She had special abilities like me," added Violet.

"Maybe her force field was turned off and she became vulnerable," returned Wendy.

"Something doesn't seem quite right," said Lexie, "may we see where she has been buried?"

"Yes of course, after school tomorrow," answered Wendy.

"I'm not going to school," said Violet.

"You have to," ordered Wendy, "there are only a few days left before you break up for the August school holidays."

"I don't feel up to school," insisted Violet.

"Either you go to school, or you both go to the Police Station," instructed mum sternly.

Violet heard a message coming through telepathically which said,

"Let's pretend we are going to school, to avoid being tagged with a tracker at the Police Station."

"Okay, we could go for a while, ditch school, find your vaccine, then go and see my dad and where they have buried Roxie Red."

"Perfect," replied Lexie.

"I have changed my mind," said Violet to her mum, "we will go to school."

The next morning, they woke to a nice hot breakfast made up of pancakes, bacon and a stream of maple syrup.

"Now eat up girls and off to school," said mum.

They both shovelled down the breakfast, drank their cups of tea and were off. The school was within walking distance, passed a row of shops.

"Those shops used to be packed with people, all doing their early morning shopping," said Violet.

"Everywhere does appear to be deserted," commented Lexie.

Violet glanced into the distance and saw several churches along with two magnificent temples.

"Why are there seven churches all lined up in a row?" asked Violet, slightly confused with the change.

"How many churches used to be there?"

"Just one," replied Violet, "everything is different from what I left. I am sure that one of those churches used to be a Bank."

They approached the school gate and Violet stopped abruptly saying,

"What's happened to my school?"

The school had electrified fencing all around, almost as though it looked like it was trying to keep kids in even though the windows had huge metal bars, leaving little room for a view out the windows.

"Are you sure that it isn't a prison?" asked Lexie with sarcasm.

They both observed their surroundings.

"It does look like a prison," remarked Violet.

They joined the queue of students lined up outside the school gate. There were several security guards searching the students. At the front of the queue, they noticed a small drone that appeared to be looking at them.

"That robot's scanning us," remarked Lexie, "do you think that it will pick up on our magical belts?"

"I guess we are about to find out," replied Violet.

The robot paused as though it had picked up a threat, but then it slowly glided to the next set of children in the queue.

"That was close," they both muttered softly.

Their next problem was getting through the security guards.

"Names please?" he asked.

Two security guards stood in front of them wearing sunglasses, so Lexie decided to communicate with Violet telepathically saying,

"Shall I just kick their ass?"

"I think that they are here to prevent trouble," replied Violet.

"Well, my name is not going to be on the list, so any bright ideas?"

"My name is Violet, and this is my cousin visiting from out of town," Violet responded to one of the security guards.

"Sorry, no visitors allowed," remarked one of the men.

"Any-more bright ideas?" Lexie asked using telekinesis.

"No," replied Violet, "any-more secret abilities?"

Lexie's head swam with thought.

"I'm a celebrity," responded Lexie, directing it towards the security guards.

Both the security guards looked directly towards Lexie in confusion. Suddenly their glasses flew off their faces and fell to the ground. Lexie and Violet seized the moment and quickly made a telepathic connection. Now under mind control, the men then stood awaiting a command.

"Now escort us into the school, please," Lexie insisted.

"I can't believe that your powers are still evolving," said Violet while the men were compelled to create a path through the students in front and lead the girls inside.

"We are in," giggled Lexie.

"Amazing," said Violet.

They walked to the reception and noticed that the girl working behind the desk was not wearing sunglasses.

"Well, this should be easy," said Lexie after staring into her eyes, blinking and making a connection.

Both girls chuckled emphatically as they were directed to Violet's morning class.

They sat down and several students piled in after them.

"Tegi," shouted Violet.

A girl with short brown hair and hazel eyes approached saying,

"Where have you been, we haven't seen you for months?"

"I've been out of town visiting family," replied Violet.

"I see you are still wearing your hair in a French plait," commented Tegi.

"This is my cousin Lexie," said Violet.

"Hope you are as bright as Violet," said Tegi, "she normally answers all the questions and that's impressive, as I'm usually the maths and science genius."

"Well, this could be a challenge," said Lexie with a confident smile.

The class was now full, and the Teacher walked in. "Hi, and good morning class, my name's Mrs Mclean."

"Good morning," the class responded.

Mrs Mclean sharply turned her head towards Lexie while saying,

"Who are you, young lady?"

Lexie stared into her eyes and smiled cheekily.

"I am Lexie."

Mrs Mclean was strangely compelled not to ask any further questions, so proceeded with instructing the class. She asked several difficult maths and science questions and Tegi was able to keep up with them for a while. After a few minutes, the questions became too difficult and only Violet and Lexie were left answering. Lexie was surprised to find the questions easy. Although violet was using 70% of her brain, she appeared to be just as advanced. After a few more minutes, Mrs Mclean gave up and the class applauded them both.

After the bell rang to signal the end of the class, Tegi joined them on their way out to break and said,

"Well, you have finally met your match, Violet."

"Yep," said Violet, "I will have to step up my game in the future."

"My brain must have really switched to digital back when Roxie gave me my enchanted belt," said Lexie proudly.

"How do you feel having an equal Violet?" Tegi asked.

"I'll kick her ass later," replied Violet in a serious tone.

Both Lexie and Tegi's face looked shocked from the unexpected response.

Outside several students joined them on the playground.

"Hi Violet, where have you been hiding?" said Merida, a Scottish girl with short light brown hair and blue eyes.

"Saving my looser cousin," replied Violet indignantly.

"What's happening to you?" asked Lexie, becoming increasingly concerned.

"Nothing," answered Violet, "I just feel a little tired."

"I'm not surprised after answering all those complex questions earlier," said Tegi.

"You were gone so long that I thought that you had moved schools," said Merida.

"We thought that we had finally got rid of you," said Brendon, an Irish kid.

"If you don't like me, then don't speak to me," responded Violet aggressively.

"She's put you in your place," interjected Lucinda, a tall, tanned girl with long silky black hair.

"Violet's not usually this moody," said Tegi.

"No, she's not," commented Lexie, "I think that there is definitely something wrong with her."

Violet suddenly pushed Lexie aggressively while saying,

"No, there's something definitely wrong with you."

Lexie refrained from responding to the threat.

"Maybe it's the increased heat from global warming," said Brendon.

"The Earth is spinning closer to the Sun these days," commented Lucinda.

"You kids have gone crazy," said Chloe, a short girl with glasses and an American accent.

"It's 7g," responded Lucinda.

"Our ancestors never took it seriously and now look at what they have caused," said Kasia, a toned Polish girl wearing a blue velvet jacket.

"I guess the convoluted conspiracy theories continued into the future," said Lexie.

"I've got a headache," informed Violet.

"Have you hit your head?" asked Lucinda with deep compassion.

"No, I don't think so," replied Violet while shaking her head.

"Maybe the jabs from the vaccinations had a negative effect on you," suggested Brendon.

"Don't speak to me," replied Violet in a nasty tone.

"I think that you had better beat it," remarked Chloe.

"She's got no right speaking to me like that," said Brendon.

"It doesn't matter who's wrong or right, just keep quiet," suggested Lucinda.

"I think that you best run and hide," advised Tegi.

"That reminds me of a song," said Lexie, now trying to calm the situation down.

"You wouldn't," said Violet.

"Why not," said Lexie, "hit it boys and girls, Lexie, music please."

Violet's mobile lit up, vibrated and then started playing music. Lexie compelled the whole playground to start singing MJ Beat it. Violet stood around watching the performance, while Lexie smiled away listening to them sing.

You better run, you better hide,

Don't be a macho man, just beat it.

Towards the end of the song, even Violet began to smile again, but their entertainment was interrupted by the sound of the school bell. They all gathered their belongings and headed into their next class. On the way in Violet screeched,

"Don't touch my mobile again or you will be sorry."

Lexie turned in fury and said,

"That's it, you're coming with me."

Lexie grabbed Violet's clothes firmly and dragged her. A teacher called Mrs Butler intercepted them and quickly said,

"Let go of that girl."

Mrs Butler was just wearing normal glasses, so Lexie used mind control and easily compelled her to show them where the girl's bathroom was situated. The Teacher turned on her heels and immediately escorted them to the bathroom.

Lexie tried the door, but it was locked.

"What is this?" asked Lexie in rage.

"You need a key for the bathroom," replied Mrs Butler.

Lexie growled in anger, spun and hit the door with a back kick, knocking it clean off its hinges.

"Leave us," Lexie yelled at the Teacher, while dragging Violet inside by her shoulder.

"Let go of me," Violet insisted.

"You better tell me what is going on before I knock you out," barked Lexie.

Violet grabbed Lexie's wrist and broke free of her hold. She twisted hard on Lexie's wrist, but she was too smart and performed a front summersault landing back on her feet. Lexie then executed a round house kick that just missed her face. The kick was so close that Violet's hair was still swaying in the breeze.

"What," said Violet looking towards her shoulder and then spinning her head back to face her little sister.

"Next time I won't miss," bellowed Lexie.

Violet moved in for the attack and they exchanged techniques with hand to hand combat. Lexie's lightning speed helped her and she easily overpowered her big sister. Violet then swung for Lexie, but her reflexes were too quick. Lexie blocked her strike and held tightly to her arm. Violet tried her hardest to break free, but Lexie held on saying,

"Tell me what's happening to you, or I'll break your wrist."

Violet then tried to rotate her wrists, but the friction began to burn her.

"What the hell," Violet complained, "you're holding me too tight."

"Stop struggling then," Lexie replied.

"Ouch, you burnt me."

"I said stop struggling."

"Why are you even holding me?" asked Violet dizzily.

"Because your emotions are getting out of hand," replied Lexie.

"Let go of me, I am in control of my emotions, remember!"

"Wait, what?" asked Lexie, now puzzled.

"Controlling your emotions is the first discipline," said Violet, "you are the one that normally struggles to control it."

"But you lost your temper in the school yard," said Lexie.

"I don't remember doing that," replied Violet.

"You were nasty towards a kid called Brendon," said Lexie.

"We are always nasty towards each other," said Violet, "it's called flirting."

"Wait, what, are you saying that you like him?"

"Yes," replied Violet with a cheerful smile.

Lexie released her grip and said, "Well, do you remember being nasty towards me?"

"No," replied Violet, "why would I do that? You are my twin sister and I love you."

"Err, what's happening here?" asked Lexie in confusion.

"You grabbed me for no reason," said Violet, "that's some Kung-Fu grip you have there."

"But, but don't you remember threatening me?"

"No," responded Violet, "let's get out of here and find your vaccine."

"Your personality has just switched."

"From what?"

"You really don't remember having an outburst?"

Violet glanced around the room and noticed the door on the floor before saying,

"No and… what happened to the bathroom door?"

"Somethings not quite right, maybe you became damaged when we emerged from the time portal."

They freshened themselves and pondered.

"Let's stop wasting time and find your vaccine to save your World."

"So, where to first?"

"UCLA campus. They have developed thousands of vaccines for deadly viruses."

"Shouldn't we change out of our school clothes first?"

Violet consulted her magical mobile and their clothes transformed into combat outfits. Then she said,

"Let's go and get your vaccine."

With that, they both slowly levitated and vanished out of sight.

Chapter 5

They re-emerged outside the gates of the UCLA University.

"Well not much has changed," expressed Lexie, "there are still 87 steps, I thought that there would be a short cut to the top."

"There is," said Violet cunningly, "follow me."

Violet levitated, floated just above the steps and glided up to the top, with Lexie following swiftly behind.

"That was much easier than walking," said Lexie cheerfully.

Glancing around, they noticed that it didn't seem very busy, a definite shortage of students.

"Can I help you?" a receptionist asked.

Violet locked eyes, blinked and said,

"Please let us in."

"Have a nice day," returned the receptionist.

She smiled cheerfully and opened the inner gates. They then walked in and headed for the South campus.

"Let's hope that there are no surprises waiting for us this time," remarked Violet.

"You said that I destroyed Dr Dre, so he can't be here, right?" asked Lexie looking for a reassuring response.

"Right, he's vapourised," replied Violet.

They walked past the water fountain and the huge statue of a bear, and they were in.

"That was easy," said Lexie as she approached the laboratory door.

"After you then," ordered Violet.

"Age before beauty," returned Lexie.

"I think that your abilities have exceeded mine," said Violet.

"Here goes then."

With that, Lexie turned the handle of the door and walked in.

Before them were several Scientists and lab assistants all busy at work.

"Where will we find the vaccine for our virus?" asked Lexie.

"You won't believe who is here," said Violet worryingly.

A girl approached. Before them now stood a tall teenage girl with long brown hair and hazel eyes.

"Can I help you girls?"

Lexie lashed out and slapped her hard across the face.

"What the hell was that for?" she screamed.

"How did you get back here?" Lexie asked.

"I work here," she replied while rubbing her jaw.

"Is your name Asha-D?"

"Yes," she replied, "what have I done to offend you?"

"Don't you remember me?" Lexie asked with fury.

Violet remained quiet for a moment.

"I've never met you before," replied Asha.

"You turned into Dr Dre," said Lexie.

"Dr Dre has not worked here for several months."

"Wait, what?" said Lexie slowly becoming hesitant.

Then a message came through telepathically from Violet saying,

"This is the real Asha-D that Dr Dre impersonated."

Lexie turned her head towards Violet to find her smiling cheekily. Then she turned back to face the girl.

"So, your name is Asha-D?"

"That's what I said," she replied.

"So… you are not Dr Dre?"

"No and I'm calling security," she insisted.

"Whoops," said Lexie.

"Slow down, slow down," interjected Violet.

The girl turned to face Violet and locked eyes. The connection was made, and Violet blinked before saying,

"Please can we have the vaccine for the influenza virus?"

Under mind control, she was compelled to agree. Asha-D smiled and said,

"Yes sure, just wait here a moment."

She rushed off, moments later re-emerging with a vial containing the vaccine.

"This will eradicate all types of influenza."

"Thanks," said Violet, taking the vile firmly into her hand and then placing it securely in her belt, "now go back to work."

"Have a great day," encouraged Asha-D who now turned away and resumed her duties.

Violet and Lexie headed out.

"Well, that was easier than I expected," said Lexie.

Outside the door they immediately encountered several Police Officers, who were all pointing their guns towards them both.

"You spoke too soon," said Violet.

A Police Officer approached and stood before them.

"You are in possession of some Government property."

"What are you talking about?" Violet asked.

"The vaccine doesn't belong to you."

Violet glanced around to see what they were up against. There were several Police dogs growling furiously and all the Officers were wearing sunglasses.

"We need this vaccine to save people's lives," said Violet.

"Hand over the vile or we will set the dogs upon you."

There was a moment of silence, while the girls contemplated their next move. Then the main Officer quickly got on his radio and called for assistance. Several more officers let loose the dogs and they began to run towards the girls. Violet jumped and performed a double inward crescent kick to both sides of the main Officer's head; he went straight down. In seconds the dogs were upon them. Lexie slapped each dog around the mouth. Then she stared into their eyes, using mind control, made a connection and said, "Go to sleep, you naughty dogs."

Both dogs tilt their heads, made a slight whimpering noise, and then fell to the ground, fast asleep. The Officers then opened fire, but the bullets bounced off their force fields, leaving the girls unharmed. Several men lunged forwards and began fighting in an unarmed combat. Both girls blocked, countered and kicked them to the ground. Another two Officers came forwards, kicking and punching. It took a second or two for Lexie and Violet to realise that they were actually fighting against female Officers.

"I can't believe they turned you girls into villains," said Lexie, finishing off her opponent with a hook punch to her jaw.

The other Officers commenced with gunfire. Several students from the University screamed in fear.

"Any ideas of how to avoid any of these innocent people from getting hurt?" asked Violet after landing from executing another jump kick.

Lexie looked up and stared towards the remaining Officers. Using her telekinesis, she compelled their sunglasses to fly away from their faces.

"Cool trick," yelled Violet.

Their eyes were revealed with just enough time for Lexie to connect with them all. They were now under mind control and compelled to follow her orders.

"Now let's have some fun," said Lexie.

"What are you going to do with them?" Violet asked.

"They all enjoy shooting," said Lexie, "so they can all sing Bang, Bang, by JJ, Lexie, music please."

Violet's mobile began to light up, vibrate and then play the musical track.

"I can't believe you are actually going to get them to sing in the middle of a gun fight," commented Violet cheerfully.

"Sing Bang, Bang, boys and girls," ordered Lexie.

The singing began.

Bang bang into the room,

Bang bang all over you,

Bang bang there goes your heart!

Students replaced their fear with joyful laughter. Officers spun and danced their way through the musical track, with Lexie and Violet just standing there, enjoying the entertainment.

"Now tell me this isn't better than having to fight and kick their asses," said Lexie triumphantly.

"Yep, it sure is," replied Violet.

At the end of the performance, Lexie yelled,

"Now everyone… take a bow and go to sleep."

There was an almighty thud and all the Officers then fell to the ground, rendered unconscious. Lexie and Violet bowed to the University students who had all started applauding. Then they casually walked off into the distance.

"You have your vaccine now, so go back and save your World," said Violet.

"What will you do?"

"I'm still gonna visit my dad in the mental hospital."

"Could I see your mum and dad before I leave?"

"Yes," said Violet, "let's get out of here."

Both girls slowly levitated and then vanished in an instant.

They reappeared outside the entrance to the Mental facility.

"That's a little risky," said Lexie, "supposing someone saw us magically appear out of thin air?"

"This is a Mental hospital," replied Violet, "they will just think that they had a hallucination."

"You know your dad's in there, right?"

"So, let's go get him out."

They entered and approached the receptionist.

"May I help you?" a man with dark hair asked.

"We have come to visit my dad," answered Violet.

"Patient's name?"

"Francisco Brooke."

"Ward 21, but it says he is not allowed visitors."

"You wouldn't deny two teenage girls their father, would you?"

Violet locked eyes, smiled and blinked. The telepathic connection was made.

"Have a great day," replied the receptionist with a bright smile.

Both girls walked down the darkly lit corridor and went to find the room. It was a large room with several patients sitting around. Two sat watching TV, a Carer was feeding one and another was rocking forwards and backwards in his seat.

"Which one's your dad?" Lexie whispered.

"The one rocking himself," replied Violet.

They walked over and stopped beside his chair. He had short dark hair and glasses.

"Dad, it's me Violet."

He continued to rock.

"It's me Violet, dad, I've returned from my time travel and journey into the past."

"Violet's gone, Violet's gone," he muttered softly to himself.

"No dad, I'm here."

He looked up and quickly recognised her big blue eyes. He smiled and said,

"Violet?"

"Yes dad, I'm alive."

"Violet alive?" he asked while slowly getting to his feet.

They embraced.

"Yes, Violet is here now, and this is Lexie."

He turned his head to face Lexie and became frightened.

"Hi," said Lexie.

"Wendy?" he asked, becoming nervous.

"My name is Lexie."

"No more, no more," he yelled frantically.

"What, people are normally happy to see me," thought Lexie disappointingly.

The carer feeding another patient quickly approached.

"What are you girls doing here?" she asked while grabbing Violet's dad and placing him back down in the chair.

"What has happened to my dad?" Violet asked with a raised voice.

"He has developed advanced dementia."

"I thought that he had a psychotic break?"

"He is also suffering from psychosis."

"What caused him to deteriorate so quickly?"

An authoritative voice came from behind yelling,

"What are you girls doing here?"

Violet turned to see a female Doctor with dark tanned skin.

"What have you butchers done with my father??"

"He has psychosis and now suffers from paranoid delusions."

"How does a top scientist, a professor, become delusional?"

"Maybe his stressful work became too much for him."

Violet's dad began to laugh and say,

"Martians live on mars."

"What did you say dad?" asked Violet.

"They're coming to get us," he yelled while rocking in his chair.

"Who?" Violet asked.

"You are all in on it," he cried.

"He is paranoid that creatures are out to get him," said the Doctor.

"What creature dad?" asked Violet.

Her dad pointed towards Lexie.

"What have I done now?" bellowed Lexie innocently.

The Doctor then said,

"You girls have scared him, please leave."

The other patients began to scream frantically. Lexie turned her head around to take a quick glance at the other patients and then said,

"The whole world has gone mad."

"Your father is hearing voices," said the Doctor, "so we have put him on antipsychotics to help his psychosis."

The Carer went to calm the other patients down.

Violet stood staring towards her father and then said, "What have they done to you?"

"He has developed Paranoia and thinks everyone is out to kill him," replied the Doctor.

"That doesn't sound like dementia," insisted Violet.

"He will forget who you are very soon," said the Doctor, "so I suggest that you both leave now."

"Can I have some privacy with him first?"

"No."

"Isn't Aerobic exercise or music good for dementia?" interjected Lexie.

"Could we take him out for a short walk?" Violet asked.

"No," insisted the Doctor.

Lexie scanned around the room and noticed a treadmill in one corner.

"He can walk on that treadmill," suggested Lexie.

Violet turned her head, glanced towards it and then faced the Doctor saying, "Two minutes on the treadmill won't harm him."

With that, Violet held firmly onto one of his arms and helped him up. Then she carefully walked him over to the treadmill and placed him securely onto it.

"Start walking dad," said Violet just as she pressed the start button.

The treadmill began to rotate slowly. Her dad began to giggle nervously as Violet pressed to go a little faster. Adrenalin began to circulate around his body, and he started to smile.

After two minutes the Doctor ordered Violet to stop the treadmill.

"Shrinks are making us out to be mad," bellowed Violet's dad.

"What do you mean?" asked Violet.

"The Government is playing mind tricks on us."

Violet pressed the stop button, helped her dad off and then took him back towards his chair.

"Is there anything you can do for him?" asked Violet in desperation.

"His condition is Irreversible," replied the Doctor.

"Please can we visit him another day?"

"Yes, but you will have to leave now, because it is time for his medication."

Lexie and Violet stood to their feet.

"Do you think that we should tell him about Red?" whispered Lexie into Violet's ear.

"Red here," blurted Violet's father.

"What?" responded Lexie in surprise.

"Roxie Red is dead," informed Violet.

"Red no dead," mumbled her dad who was starting to quickly rock once more.

"It's time for you both to leave," said the Doctor who was now trying to quickly usher them out.

Lexie touched Francisco's shoulder to say goodbye. She suddenly felt a rush of red images in her head that looked like a girl. Then she saw an image of herself, which quickly faded away. Lexie was deeply troubled with the experience but kept quiet until they both were outside the entrance to the hospital.

"You're quiet," said Violet.

"I think that I just had a premonition," said Lexie nervously.

"What did you see?" Violet asked.

"I think that I just saw Roxie Red."

"What do you mean?" asked Violet.

"I think that Red is still alive."

Chapter 6

Violet stood there in silence, still in shock at the chance of Red being still alive.

"Could you see where she is being kept?"

"I sensed that she is being kept captive in a secret lab and they are performing experiments on her."

"Do you think that she is here in Los Angeles?"

"No, there was an awful lot of red, so I think that she is more likely to be held somewhere in Russia."

"Was she harmed?"

"She appeared weak or in pain."

"If she is held in a top-secret location, I am going to need some help finding her."

"Don't worry, I will help you."

"No, you need to get that vaccine back to your World."

"I would like to help in finding Roxie Red first, please."

"I think that we need the rest of the Rainbow girls."

"Have you tried contacting them using your telekinesis again?"

"Yes, but I am getting nothing."

"Call one of them and see if I can help using my new power."

Lexie stared towards Violet's mobile in her left palm and heard something strange. It sounded like someone skimming quickly through a large book, from front to back.

"Helen's not responding," said Violet.

"I heard something," said Lexie.

"What did you hear?"

"I'm not sure, but I sensed that Helen is in Arizona."

"Wait, what?" asked Violet, now baffled.

"I guess I have the power to decipher digital signals," smiled Lexie, "now, let's go find our girl."

"We should inform my mother first, so that she does not worry about us running off to Arizona, when we should be in school."

When they arrived back at Violet's home, her mum Wendy was on her mobile. They walked in and she quickly hung up saying,

"What are you girls doing here, when you should be in school?"

"Red is not dead," said Violet.

"She is dead, I attended her funeral."

"Lexie says she had a premonition that she is still alive."

Wendy gazed towards Lexie with interest.

"Do you have the ability to have premonitions?" Wendy asked.

"Yes," replied Lexie with a cheerful smile.

"Since when?"

"Since I arrived in this World."

"So, your abilities are growing?"

"I guess so, yes."

"We need to go to Arizona to find Helen," interjected Violet.

"Why would you do that?" Wendy asked.

"To gather the Rainbow girls to help us find Red."

Violet's mum paused in thought.

"You both need to have your trackers installed at the Police Station first."

"We haven't got time," answered Violet.

"Arizona is over four hundred miles away, let me fly you there."

"We could fly faster."

"You don't want anyone to see you flying, so why not take the magna train?"

"That would take over four hours," said Lexie.

"Magnetic trains are much faster now dear," said Wendy, "HS3 Zion trains travel at the speed of sound, so could get you there in less than half an hour."

"Four hundred miles in half an hour; wow, that's fast," commented Lexie.

"Let me pack you some lunch and take you to the Train Station," insisted Wendy.

"Okay mum," Violet agreed while glancing down towards her helpless dog Orion.

Just outside their town was the Zion Train Station. Wendy purchased two tickets and saw them off.

"Good luck girls," said Wendy as they got on board.

They sat down strapped themselves in and started eating their pack lunch, while the train slightly lifted off the track and began to glide away.

"Are you telling me that this HS3 train travels at over seven hundred miles an hour?"

"I guess so," replied Violet.

"Wow," repeated Lexie whilst sipping on her Tea.

Ten minutes into their journey Lexie remembered something quite disturbing.

"You know that I am now able to tune into mobile frequencies?"

"Yes."

"Well, I think that I heard something strange when we walked into your house."

"What did you hear?"

"I think that your mum was on the phone to the Government."

"Probably complaining about the bills or something," said Violet.

"It sounded like she was complaining that they lost something valuable."

"Like what?"

"The other person on the phone said - We failed to contain the Asset."

Violet thought for a second and then said,

"Oh no, we forgot to tell her that we visited dad."

They sat in silence sipping on their tea.

Fifteen minutes into the journey and they felt a slight jolt.

"Is that supposed to happen at this speed?" asked Lexie worryingly.

"No, it guarantees a smooth ride every time," replied Violet.

"Sounds like our trains from my World, always late but they will get you there!" Lexie remarked sarcastically.

But then there was another slight jolt and some people around began to murmur frantically.

"Somethings not quite right," said Violet, "can you try and tune into the train driver?"

Lexie closed her eyes and concentrated. After a few seconds she opened her eyes as though she had a fright.

"It's bad," exclaimed Lexie.

"What did you hear?"

"The train driver is no longer in control, because someone has managed to override their system."

"You mean we are on a runaway train?" Violet asked.

"Yes, out of control and travelling at the speed of sound," Lexie replied.

Violet turned her head to see people beginning to hold tightly to one another in desperate fear of their lives.

"What are we going to do?"

"Whatever can we do at this speed?" asked Lexie.

"You're the Brainiac," said Violet, looking slightly worried.

Lexie glanced around frantically, looking for something that might assist them. She was then compelled to look up at the TV screen. There staring back at her was the face of… Dr Dre.

"Look at the monitors," said Lexie in haste.

Violet turned her head and froze for a second, then slowly said,

"Can you see Dr Dre?"

"Yes," replied Lexie.

"It's got to be an illusion," said Violet.

"I hope that it is just in our heads," said Lexie.

The face on the TV screens began to smile and then it spoke out saying,

"So you both made it back, well this is my World and I am in control now."

"What are we going to do?" Lexie whispered.

Violet listened to the voice as it continued to speak.

"I am in control of this train now and in twenty minutes it will crash at the speed of sound."

People on the train began to scream in hysterics.

"What do you want us to do?" asked Violet.

"Take off your belts and hand them over to my men and everyone will live."

Several Police Officers approached.

"And if we don't?" asked Violet.

"Then you can either fly off or die with everyone else on the train."

Dr Dre began to cackle nastily.

Lexie remained silent for a moment.

"Any bright ideas?" asked Violet.

"I'm thinking," replied Lexie.

"Well hurry," said Violet who had just sprung to her feet in preparation for a battle.

"We'll fight our way to the front of the train and then resume control," responded Lexie.

Violet started fighting with two Officers, while Lexie casually scraped her hair back and put it neatly in a hair band.

"Where were you?" asked Violet, breathing heavily as she finished them both off.

"I was busy doing my hair."

The girls walked into the next train carriage and were confronted by some more Police Officers, who immediately commenced with gunfire. The bullets deflected off their invisible force fields, while other passengers screamed in fright. Lexie threw one over her shoulder for Violet to finish off, while she kicked and punched two more. There was just one left and he decided to stop shooting. Lexie approached him and stood before him. He pointed the gun directly towards her head and said,

"Take off your belt and give up or I'll blow your head off."

"Do you really think that you are quicker than me?" asked Lexie in a serious tone.

The gun fired and people screamed, but Lexie still stood before him. Then she opened her hand and he saw the bullet.

"What the hell are you?"

"We are the Rainbow girls," replied Lexie while executing a front kick into his groin.

He went down groaning in pain.

They walked into the next carriage and were confronted with two men holding people at gunpoint in front of them.

"Give up or we will shoot these innocent passengers."

Lexie heard a message from Violet using her telekinesis saying,

"You take off their sunglasses and I will compel them using mind control."

The girls acted in perfect teamwork. In a split second, their sunglasses flew off, the guns fell to the ground along with the two men, who were now fast asleep.

Two more carriages to go before they reached the front, but there stood before them were four Police Officers holding hand grenades.

"Take one more step towards us and we will set these hand grenades off and blow up everyone on this train."

Lexie heard another message coming through telepathically.

"How fast are you?"

"Faster than a bullet, why?"

"Do you think that you are fast enough to take two grenades out of the hand of the two Officers on my right?"

"Yep, and you'll take the other two, right?"

"No, I'll take the two on my left."

"That's what I said," replied Lexie.

"No time for jokes, are you ready?" Violet asked.

"I was born ready," Lexie responded.

"After three, one… two… three."

There was no movement. Both girls still stood before the Officers as they glanced around in sheer confusion of where their hand grenades had suddenly disappeared to.

"Looking for these boys?" Lexie asked while opening her hand to reveal two hand grenades perfectly intact.

Both girls then placed the hand grenades safely into their magical belts, which automatically disarmed them. Suddenly the Officers sunglasses flew off their faces and then both men tumbled to the ground unconscious, while the passengers clapped their hands in joy of still being alive.

They made their way into the final carriage and were met with something completely different. Several small robots were crawling around the carriage floor.

"What in God's creatures is that?" asked Lexie while staring down towards one.

"Replicators," said Violet.

"What can they do?" Asked Lexie.

"Don't let them touch you or they will inject you with poison," advised Violet.

The girls darted around the carriage avoiding the sharp spikes on the ends. The replicators chased them wherever they went. Replicators jumped like giant spiders at their faces, but the girls swiftly manoeuvred out of the line of fire. After a short while, two replicators grew, produced skin and transformed into copies of both Lexie and Violet.

"Wait, what!" yelled Lexie.

"Oh yeah, they are self-replicating entities that can replicate humans," advised Violet.

"How are we supposed to know who the real deal is?" asked Lexie, now fighting against a carbon copy of herself.

"Trust your instincts."

They fought on, sometimes fighting against a clone of themselves and other times fighting against the carbon copy of the other person. After a few minutes it became a little confusing and Lexie gave the real Violet a right hook.

"It's me," yelled Violet.

"Whoops, sorry, I got a little carried away," replied Lexie.

After another minute, the girls managed to overpower the replicators and three clones of themselves now lay helpless on the floor. The carbon copies then slowly turned back into small replicators and then melted away, vanishing as though they were never there.

The girls opened the driver's door and walked in.

"What are you girls doing here?"

"We have come to help," answered Violet.

"I don't think that two teenagers are able to help our situation," he remarked.

"You will be surprised what we are capable of," said Lexie.

"Unless you can come up with a way of stopping this train, then you are no good to me."

"Why? Doesn't the brakes work?" asked Violet.

"Nothing works. Someone has overridden the controls."

"Can't we smash the circuits and force it to stop?" Lexie suggested.

A familiar voice came onto the TV screen and said,

"I am in control of this train now."

The driver stared into the face on the screen and then said,

"Who is he?"

"That's Dr Dre and he is a homicidal maniac," said Violet.

"He will not think twice about killing everyone on board this train," added Lexie.

"God help us," said the train driver brushing a hand through his greasy brown hair.

"If you girls try to stop the train, there is another train coming from behind in a few minutes and it will crash into you at the speed of sound."

Dr Dre cackled.

"That will kill innocent people," shouted Lexie.

"There's no way out. Either hand over your magical belts or everyone on this train dies."

"How many passengers are on this train?" whispered Violet.

"Hundreds," replied the driver.

"If we stop, there's no way we can evacuate that many people and get them far enough away, to avoid getting harmed from the wreckage of the crash," commented Lexie.

"If we had a way of speeding up the train to nine hundred miles an hour, the system would automatically shut down, then reboot and lock out the criminal," suggested the driver.

"How can we do that?" asked Violet.

"I don't know, but we will then kill hundreds more people waiting on the Arizona Train Station platform, which is just five minutes away."

"Are you telling me that we only have a five-minute window?" asked Lexie in a raised voice.

"There is a small train on the train track in front," interjected Dr Dre, "you are due to collide with it in three minutes."

He laughed some more.

"Is he serious?" asked Violet.

The driver glanced at his controls and then said,

"I'm afraid he is telling the truth. There is an obstacle on the train track ahead."

"We are trapped," concluded Violet.

Chapter 7

L exie glanced out of the front window while her head swam with thought. After making her final decision, she said,

"I will just have to speed this train up."

"How? We are no longer in control," said the driver.

"How tough is the glass in the front window?"

"It can withstand speeds of up to one thousand miles per hour and then it will shatter," replied the driver.

"Please tell all the passengers to have their seat belts on," ordered Lexie.

The Driver relayed the message on his Tannoy system, while the girls discussed their plans.

"What on Earth are you going to do girl?" asked Violet.

"I'm going to fly this train."

"Is she serious?" asked the driver, turning his head nervously towards Violet and staring directly into her eyes.

"Yes," replied Violet.

"Oh yeah, dispose of these," said Lexie handing the driver two neutralised grenades out of her belt.

"Err, what are those?" asked the driver in a slight panic.

"Don't worry, they have all been disarmed," replied Violet who was now reaching into her belt to retrieve two more.

"Keep your eyes on your controls and relay any speed changes," said Lexie just as she floated off the ground and slowly hovered towards the front window screen.

She then rotated horizontally and grabbed the front screen with both hands. The amber crystal gemstone on her belt lit up and her hands became securely fastened to the screen. Violet and the train driver watched the speedometer on the controls. It was travelling at a steady seven hundred and sixty seven miles per hour, the speed of sound. Then, almost magically, the speed began to rise.

"My God," said the train driver incredulously, "she's doing it."

The train accelerated, hitting eight hundred and then eight hundred and fifty miles per hour.

"Come on girl," encouraged Violet nervously, "you can do it."

"You need to remove the train from the train track in front," instructed Lexie.

"I'm on it," replied Violet while levitating and then she disappeared, teleporting onto the other small train.

The train driver looked over his shoulder, but there was no sign of Violet.

"Incredible," muttered the driver softly.

In a split second, Violet had reappeared on the small train.

"Where did you come from?" asked the other driver.

"No time for questions," said Violet, "there is a HS3 train approaching at the speed of sound, so you need to put this in reverse quickly."

"How is that possible?"

"There is no time to argue," yelled Violet, "just do it, now!"

The train Driver looked at his controls and realised that Violet was telling the truth and in less than one minute they would collide.

Meanwhile Lexie sped up once more to eight hundred and seventy miles an hour.

"You're not going to do it," bellowed the driver, "we are going to collide in forty seconds."

"Then hold on tightly," said Lexie just as they reached nine hundred miles an hour.

"The system has shut down with ten seconds left, but what about the other train?" asked the Driver.

"I said hold on tightly," repeated Lexie just as the train began to lift off the track.

"What's happening?" asked the driver, now becoming a little baffled.

"We are flying," answered Lexie.

There was a loud noise that sounded like thunder that could be heard on the small train.

"What on God's Earth was that?"

"I think that was the sound of a flying train," replied Violet with a smile, "she did it."

Lexie glided high above the train track heading for the Arizona Train Station.

"The system has rebooted and there is no sign of any interference."

Dr Dre suddenly noticed that he had lost connection and was no longer in control.

"Arghh," he growled in frustration.

"How will you reduce your speed and slow down to return the train back onto the train track?" asked the train driver, glancing upwards to a teenage girl who was apparently just floating in thin air.

Lexie slightly reduced her speed and felt a slight jolt. She then sent a telepathic message to Violet saying,

"I'm gonna need help keeping this train steady while I touch back down."

Violet disappeared just as the other driver asked her if she knew who was flying the other train. He looked over his shoulder, but the mysterious blond girl had vanished.

Violet reappeared just behind the flying train. She glided in, held onto the back of the train and relayed messages to Lexie using telekinesis.

"Hold it steady as I slow down," said Lexie.

She worked with Violet and synchronised a rescue, slowing the train down as it glided closer to the track.

"The system says we are thirty seconds from passing through the train station," said the worried train driver.

The girls slowed down some more, at the same time as keeping the whole train perfectly straight.

"Now it says we are ten seconds from the train station."

The girls slowed the train down enough to glide down to a stop just before carefully pulling into the Arizona Train Station, with only a few seconds left. People on the platform watched as a train seemed to hover and then glide to a stop.

Passengers clapped their hands and jeered, while the two girls slowly floated onto the platform. They then casually walked through the crowd of passengers and made their quick exit.

"We did it," said Lexie smiling victoriously.

"No, you did it, you saved everybody," complimented Violet.

"Where to now?" asked Lexie while fixing her hair straight.

"Let's go find our sister Helen."

"Follow me," said Lexie as they vanished.

They followed her directions and teleported to the front gate of Helen's house.

"How are you so accurate with your predictions?" asked Violet.

"I can sense where the other end of a phone call leads by tracking its digital signal."

Violet opened the door to the house and hastily walked in. There, curled up on a sofa was Helen, in a romantic embrace.

"Sorry to interrupt you," said Violet.

Helen released her lock on his lips and turned to face her sisters.

"What are you two doing here?"

"We have come to take you back to Los Angeles," replied Lexie.

"Can't you see I'm busy?" said Helen, resuming her affectionate embrace.

"Who is that?" asked Violet.

"This is Daniel-son, my Karate kid."

Helen then chopped him in the head to be friendly, but her Karate chop was a little too hard.

"Ouch," moaned Daniel who started rubbing his sore head.

Lexie glanced at Daniel and then turned her head towards Helen. "Sorry to cut your passion short, but we have a mission to go on."

"I'm not going anywhere," said Helen, "since Red died, we have disbanded the Rainbow girls. You two have been gone for months, so we have all gone our own way and have different lives now."

"We think that Red is still alive," said Violet.

"She's dead, I attended her funeral."

"Did you see her in the coffin?" asked Lexie.

"Yes."

Violet turned her head to face Lexie and said,

"Maybe you are wrong, maybe she really is dead."

"No," Lexie responded, "I trust my instincts, something isn't quite right."

Helen cuddled Daniel-Son for comfort.

"Well Dr Dre is still alive," said Violet.

"How do you know for sure?" asked Helen.

"I heard his voice on the phone and then he tried to crash our train," replied Lexie.

"Are you sure he wasn't just a figment of your imagination?" Helen asked.

"That's what I thought at first," said Violet, "but I have seen him too. He came onto the TV screens on the train and threatened to crash the train unless we handed over our enchanted belts."

"But you destroyed him," said Helen, turning to face Lexie.

"I did, but he is back."

There was silence for a few seconds. Then Violet continued and said, "We know that he is alive, because he sent people to kill us on the train. We had to fight them off. He even sent replicators after us. Then Lexie had to make the HS3 Train fly to avoid a crash."

"Please tell me you are joking?" asked Helen, becoming more interested in the conversation.

"The replicators transformed into clones of us, and we had to fight them off."

"But then they disappeared, or they are able to teleport like us," added Lexie.

"Replicators that look like us?" Helen asked.

"Yes," said Lexie.

"Did you call the Police?"

"No," said Violet, "they are working for Dr Dre. There were several Police Officers attacking us on the train."

"They were also trying to kill us or test the level of our special abilities at the Police Station," said Lexie.

"How?" asked Helen.

"They shot us, tried to blow us up with hand grenades and then electrified the floor," replied Lexie.

"But Lexie ran faster than the pressure plates could sense us," added Violet.

"I can't believe that the Police are corrupt," expressed Helen.

Daniel-Son refrained from getting involved with the conversation and sat playing on his mobile phone, like a typical boy!

"You have to come and help us so that Lexie can return back to her World," said Violet.

"What took you so long to travel here through the time portal?" asked Helen.

"We followed you through the portal just a few minutes after you and the rest of the Rainbow girls left," replied Violet.

"I don't see how that is anatomically possible," said Helen, now looking quite baffled.

"I think that Dr Dre has damaged the very fabric of time," said Lexie.

"Does anyone know what his intentions are?"

"No," said Lexie, "but I think that it has something to do with Roxie."

"What makes you think that?"

"We went to see my dad in a psychiatric hospital and-"

"What is your dad doing in the hospital?" interjected Helen.

"He is suffering from psychosis or dementia, I don't really know, it all sounds dodgy, but then Lexie had a premonition that she saw Roxie alive."

"Is this a new ability?" asked Helen.

"Yes, my powers are evolving."

"Do you think that you can use your telekinesis to relay the memory to us?" asked Helen.

"I can give it a try," replied Lexie.

She then went quiet, concentrating on previous memories and hoping that both Violet and Helen could picture what she was seeing in her mind. A few seconds later, Helen's eyes widened as though she had a fright.

"Red is trapped and hurt," said Helen.

"I saw the images too," said Violet, "if those flashing memories are true, then Red is indeed still alive and has been held in a top-secret location, where she is unable to use her powers."

They stood around for a moment, contemplating their next move. Then Lexie had an idea.

"Violet, did you say that you can see through walls?"

"Yes, why?"

"We could go to where Red has been buried and you could scan the grounds and see if her body is still there."

"Okay, let's go," said Violet.

There was no response from Helen.

"Are you coming too?" Lexie grovelled.

Helen stood quiet, her mind swimming with thought.

"Please Helen," pleaded Violet, "one last mission, if Roxie is dead, then you can come back and resume your life here with Daniel-Son."

Helen glanced towards Daniel, he smiled back passionately. Then she said, "Okay, you two wait outside and I will just say goodbye to my Daniel-Son."

Three minutes later Helen joined them outside. She held up her left hand to reveal her mobile in her palm and called,

"Lexie."

Her mobile began to flash all sorts of beautiful colours and then her clothes quickly changed into her red, white and blue all American combat outfit with a sequence of stars.

"So, are you ready?" Violet asked.

"Let's go," replied Helen.

They started to walk off and then Lexie said,

"Err, where are we going?"

"We are catching the high-speed train back to Los Angeles."

"Err, we had a bad experience on your train, so we would rather fly, thanks," commented Lexie sarcastically.

"Trains rarely crash these days," said Helen.

"I think that flying is always the safest way to travel!" remarked Violet.

They turned a corner and then vanished. Seconds later they reappeared from their teleportation, landing just outside the cemetery.

It looked spooky, but then it was a cemetery full of deceased bodies. They slowly walked in and followed Helen to where they had previously buried Red.

"Here she is," said Helen, "looks just like we left it three months ago. I can't see any signs of anyone tampering with the grave. She left us too soon. Eighteen is far too young to die."

"Over to you, Violet," said Lexie.

Violet looked down towards the grave and concentrated hard. The flowers, the grass and the ground through her eyes disappeared and she saw dirt. Using her thermal imaging abilities, she scanned deeper and now she was able to see the wooden coffin.

"Well?" Helen asked.

The coffin appeared glossy white. Inside was covered in beautiful red velvet.

"Do you see anything?" asked Lexie.

"No," replied Violet.

"What do you mean no?" asked Helen.

"I mean… the casket is empty," replied Violet.

It was a red padded cell, one made to keep patients from harming themselves. The room was dimly lit with a dull red light. There were two women sprawled across the dirty floor. One girl was young, with long red hair, wearing a familiar red hooded cloak, but no sign of a belt. They both looked malnourished, as though they hadn't eaten for months. Then the door opened, and someone entered and slowly walked over to the girl dressed in red.

After a few seconds they said, "My child, it's time for your tonic."

Chapter 8

They stood around, still in shock of the absence of Red in her casket. Helen spoke first saying,

"I saw her with my own eyes lying there in the coffin. Then they closed it and lowered her into the ground. I don't understand, where could she have disappeared to?"

There was silence while both Lexie and Violet ran over different scenarios in their mind. Then Lexie had a brain wave and said, "Didn't the clone replicators of us on the Train disappear?"

Violet turned to face Lexie and said,

"Are you saying they buried a clone replicator of Red?"

"Yes," Lexie nodded.

"So where is the real Roxie Red?" Helen asked.

Helen paced up and down, still feeling overwhelmed with the details she had just learnt.

"We need to trace her last steps and find out where she might be held."

"Shall we start with her family in Russia?" asked Lexie.

"Yes, that's a good place to start," replied Helen.

"Are you ready to teleport to Russia?" Violet asked.

They all nodded their heads, slowly floated off the ground and were gone.

In a flash, they arrived outside Roxie Red's parent's house in St Petersburg in Russia and knocked the door.

"Does anyone speak Russian?" Lexie asked while the door opened.

"We all speak several languages," replied Helen.

Speaking in Russian, the man asked them who they were. Violet answered and had a conversation, before Roxie's mum appeared. Helen joined in and they were then invited in. While Roxie's parents prepared some authentic Russian food, Lexie said,

"I really need to learn Russian."

Violet turned to face her and said,

"Look into my eyes."

Lexie stared into her big blue eyes.

"Now do you trust me?"

Lexie nodded. The connection was made. Lexie then felt a little nervous remembering having a head rush last time she was asked to stare into Violet's eyes. She heard a whistling noise, but no head rush.

"Didn't it work this time?" asked Lexie.

Violet spoke in Russian and asked Lexie if she had ever travelled to Russia before. She was surprised to understand every word.

"So now I know Russian?" asked Lexie in her new language, with a joyful smile.

"You can speak several languages," replied Violet cheerfully.

"What?" asked Lexie.

"I downloaded the contents of our entire library into your mind."

"Cool, so now I am bilingual."

Roxie Red's parents dressed the dinner table and then asked them to come and sit. They all ate happily while continuing the conversation in Russian. Lexie asked questions of what Red did on her last day with them. They explained that she had prepared her suitcase for her holiday with her friends, but they were not sure who she went on holiday with. Red's parents invited them to stay overnight and prepared to take them out for some entertainment. Red's mum fetched a fluffy hat and furry coat for them all. Then they went out and danced to traditional Russian music.

The next day they decided to fly off to Switzerland, where Roxie Red had gone on holiday and where she had her skiing accident. The snow was thick and cold, even for three girls with superpowers. They entered the hotel in the Swiss Alps and requested to speak to the manager. He spoke in German and told them of the accident but said that he was told that there was an avalanche and that she had been trapped in the snow before losing her life.

"I thought that your mum said that she had hit a tree?" asked Lexie slightly puzzled with the detail.

"She did," replied Violet.

"So then how did she die?" asked Lexie.

"You should know," answered the Manager.

"What do you mean?" asked Helen with widened eyes.

The Manager pointed directly towards Lexie and then said,

"You were with her."

They all turned towards Lexie and stared into her face with confusion.

"Wait, what! I wasn't there," Lexie responded in defence.

"Then it was somebody that looked remarkably similar to you," returned the Manager.

Nobody spoke for a second or two. Then Violet said,

"Do you think that it could have been my mum on holiday with Red?"

Outside the hotel, the three girls contemplated their next move.

"This is getting weird," said Lexie.

"Why wouldn't mum say she was there when Red was supposed to have died?"

"Maybe she has something to hide," said Helen.

"Or maybe she had something to do with her death or her disappearance," added Lexie.

"Either way, we need to confront her," said Violet.

"Not yet," advised Lexie, "let's get more proof first."

"Why don't you two go and find the other Rainbow girls for backup and I will go undercover and secretly follow her?" suggested Helen.

"That's a plan," agreed Lexie.

"Be careful," advised Violet, "if my mum has anything to do with Red's disappearance, then she could be potentially dangerous."

They all slowly levitated and then disappeared. Helen emerged outside Violet's house, while the other two teenage girls appeared outside the Bruno gym in Las Vegas.

"Are you sure Tamir is here?"

"This is where I sensed your mobile signal disconnected," replied Lexie.

Both girls wandered inside the building and glanced around. A tall girl with dark tanned skin stood in the distance speaking on a microphone. Then Violet sent her a message using telekinesis and she came running over.

"What are you girls doing here?" an excited Tamir asked whilst giving them a warm embrace.

"We have just travelled back through the portal," replied Violet.

"What took you girls so long?"

"Dr Dre has damaged the very fabric of time and the Universe," answered Lexie, "so even though we left minutes after you, we only just arrived."

"You mean that you have been travelling through the gateway for months?"

"Yes," said Lexie.

"Is the gateway even still open?" Tamir asked.

"We will find out when Lexie travels back in time, but first we have another problem to solve," said Violet.

"What's that?"

"Dr Dre survived."

"No way," Tamir gasped, "I saw you blow him into a million pieces."

"He's alive," said Lexie, "and Red is still alive too."

"Girl, you better not be playing," Tamir replied.

"We need your help," said Lexie.

"To do what?"

"To find out whose idea it was to pretend Red is dead and to find out where they are holding her captive."

Tamir thought for a while. She peered over her shoulder at all the noise that was becoming progressively louder.

"I've got too much going on here," Tamir reported.

"What are you even doing here?" asked Lexie.

"I am the Coordinator for the Bruno gyms."

"What's that?"

"Bruno is a franchise, it's a gym now available in most popular cities around the World."

"To help who?"

"Our organisation promotes peace, supports people with mental health issues and we also put on fighting exhibitions."

"Sounds like hard work," said Lexie.

"I'll tell you what," challenged Tamir, "if you can beat my girls, then I will come with you to find Red."

Lexie turned to glance down to the huge ring, which had several flood lights converging onto the canvas. There were several girls entering, accompanied by music and dancing, all dressed in glamorous fighting outfits. Lexie then turned to face Violet and said, "What about you?"

"You're on your own girl," replied Violet with her usual cheeky smile.

Lexie stared towards the ring, which was glowing brightly from the colourful fluorescent lights. She then turned her head to face Tamir.

"How many do I have to beat?"

"Today it's called Queen of the ring, so there's eight girls to knock out."

"Can I at least go and get changed first?"

"No, you look good in your combat outfit."

Lexie took another good look at her eight challengers, all standing in the ring awaiting the bell.

"Go get your things ready," said Lexie, "this won't take long."

Tamir gave her a huge smile and then announced a new challenger that would be entering the ring.

Spectators calmed down and became silent. The eight girls all turned and looked Lexie directly in the face.

"Is this a joke?" asked a huge, toned Russian girl with long golden hair that looked like she was in her thirties.

"She's just a teenager," said Kiera, a black girl dressed in pink.

Lexie casually wandered into the ring and stood facing all eight girls.

"So is it free for all, or do I take all eight of you on at the same time?" said Lexie while neatly tying her hair up using a strand from either side.

The other girls laughed hysterically. Then Tamir rang the bell and the fight was on.

The huge toned Russian girl called Goldilocks, approached and towered over Lexie. She was dressed in a red cape and long black boots with silver sparkles all over her face.

"You are nothing but a child," said Goldilocks, "I have been Queen of the ring champion for years. How are you supposed to beat me? Maybe you should go back home to your momma."

"Maybe you should return to your tower, Goldilocks," Lexie confidently responded.

"One teenager against eight of the most fearsome females in the World. How are…"

"Must you talk so much or are we going to fight?" Lexie interjected.

The Russian girl pushed Lexie and Lexie pushed her right back. Then the Russian girl grabbed one of Lexie's arms and pulled her hard, so that she bounced off the ropes. When Lexie collided with her, they both slightly staggered backwards. Goldilocks stared down at Lexie's magical belt and said, "So you have something under your belt do yah?"

Goldilocks ran past Lexie and continued to bounce hard off the ropes to give her an increase off momentum. Lexie followed, bouncing off the opposite rope and they met once again in the middle. They collided but neither moved. Then Lexie quickly performed a Judo throw, first grabbing Goldilocks's arm and then throwing her over her shoulder and down to the canvas. The other girls watched in amazement and the crowd went wild.

"Who's next?" asked Lexie victoriously.

A pretty girl called Phoebe, dressed similar to a witch approached. She had long mat black hair and a pale white face. Her black outfit had a picture of a cute cat smiling happily.

"Oh, I'm scared," murmured Lexie.

"You should be," said Phoebe.

Sparks of light beamed from one of her hands and hit Lexie, knocking her to the floor.

"What!" bellowed Lexie turning her head quickly to face Tamir, "you didn't say they had powers."

Tamir and Violet giggled joyfully from the ring side.

"Do you want some more little girl?" said Phoebe, preparing to fire once again.

"Bring it witch!" replied Lexie now with her force field up.

More sparks were seen as the beam of light reflected off Lexie and bounced back hitting Phoebe across the ring and onto the canvas, rendered unconscious. The crowd of spectators watching jeered loudly.

Kiera approached looking quite toned.

"I bet that hurt," she bellowed towards Phoebe.

Lexie stood firmly ready for a fight.

"Do you want some?"

"Tough little girl, aren't you?" asked Kiera.

"Yep," returned Lexie.

"Do you really think that you are able to overpower eight of us? We have been fighting each other for years and nobody can beat us when we team up together."

"Do all you girls talk too much?" asked Lexie cheekily.

"So, you want a piece of me?"

Just then, Lexie heard some shuffling behind her. She turned to see another girl ducking down low. She rugby tackled Lexie and pinned her to the canvas.

"Where did you come from?" said Lexie, now grappling on the floor.

"Meet Dominoah," Kiera laughed, "now that's what we call teamwork."

She then piled on top of Lexie and they both began to shower her with blows, whilst wrestling on the ring floor. After a short moment of grappling, Lexie levitated and floated off the canvas. She rose horizontally to the height of three metres. Kiera and Dominoah both gazed down at the mat in fear. Lexie broke loose from their holds and threw them off. They both tried hanging on, but soon fell hard back down on the floor.

Lexie swooped swiftly down, landing in front of Goldilocks, who had risen back to her feet. Goldilocks executed a hard punch to Lexie's torso with no effect.

"Have you got a brick wall under your top?" Goldilocks asked, shaking her hand in pain from the impact.

This time Lexie grabbed her arm and threw her across the ring. She bounced off the rope and hurtled back towards Lexie. Thinking fast, Lexie jumped and connected with her face using both feet. Spectators shouted with joy. Goldilocks flew back and landed on her back in pain. Dominoah rugby tackled Lexie once more. Her reflexes were too quick for Dominoah and Lexie first picked her up in a horizontal position, then slammed her back down on the canvas hard. She landed on her face and was knocked out cold. Lexie turned her over to make sure. Dominoah, a half Indian and Portuguese girl, was out of the fight. She then dragged her to the edge and rolled her off the canvas.

Kiera was back and proceeded to clobber at Lexie's face with her forearm. Lexie blocked a strike and held on tightly. The girl unknowingly looked into Lexie's green eyes and Lexie gazed right back. She blinked, the psychic connection was made, and Kiera stopped in her tracks, hypnotised and awaiting further instructions.

"Now let's have a little fun," said Lexie turning to face Jet, a Japanese girl that was running in for a fight, "Kiera, you attack her."

Lexie pointed towards Jet. Kiera turned and started punching Jet, who looked half French with her olive tanned skin.

Two more girls attacked Lexie. In complete surprise, she said,

"Rachel, Rebecca, what are you doing here?"

"We don't know you," the twin girls replied while punching and kicking.

"Are you telling me that even your descendants hate me?" replied Lexie whilst defending herself.

"I have never met you before," said Rachel.

Lexie blocked an attack and picked Rachel up. Then she just tossed her out of the ring like a tennis ball. Spectators screamed.

"Sorry Rachel," bellowed Lexie, now turning to face Rebecca.

"You are going to pay for hurting my twin sister," said Rebecca, now pushing and shoving Lexie's shoulders hard.

"I thought that you were the nice twin, please don't let me have to hurt you," pleaded Lexie.

Suddenly a girl grabbed Lexie from the rear. She was strong and held on tightly. Lexie stared into Rebecca's eyes, blinked and made a psychic connection.

"You're finished little girl," said Goldilocks who managed to hold on.

"Rebecca, help me," instructed Lexie.

Under mind control and unable to withstand her order, Rebecca proceeded to fight with Goldilocks. Lexie broke free and watched as they fought each other.

"Leave my friend alone," yelled Rebecca towards Goldilocks.

Lexie rubbed her hands together twice and said,

"Job done."

A Chinese girl called Dragon, kicked Lexie from the rear. She staggered forwards before turning to face her. The girl had a huge picture of a red dragon across her top. She came in fast, showering Lexie with Wing-Chun Kung Fu. Lexie blocked and countered. For a few seconds, they exchanged blows with hand-to-hand combat. Dragon then performed an aerial kick and knocked Lexie to the canvas.

"Sorry but here's 80% of my skills," said Lexie, speeding up to an unmanageable velocity.

Dragon was unable to keep up and was soon flying across the ring. She bounced off the ropes and headed back towards Lexie. As she came in close, Lexie jumped and spun around, executing a spinning heel kick. It connected and the girl was down, but not out.

A chair was smashed against Lexie's head. Spectators screamed in disappointment now taking a liking towards her.

"That could have really hurt," said Lexie, turning around to face Goldilocks who had just beaten Rebecca.

She still had the chair in her hands, preparing for another strike. Lexie lunged forwards, executing another spinning heel kick. It connected with the chair and smashed it to pieces. Crowds of people began to clap their hands cheerfully. Goldilocks was surprised to only see one leg of the chair left in her hand. She performed a strike, but Lexie blocked it. Lexie then picked her up and turned her upside down in her arms. She slightly floated off the ring floor and then came back down, hitting her head hard against the canvas like a tombstone. Goldilocks was out cold.

Phoebe the witch was back up and flying around the ring on a broomstick. She landed on the top rope and balanced with the broomstick held horizontal in both hands. Lexie took a run up and jumped. She used the ropes of the ring to gather more height, as she literally ran vertically upwards. After grabbing the stick, she kicked the witch off the rope and then somersaulted back down to the canvas. Phoebe The witch landed outside the ring, flat out on her back unconscious. Lexie turned around victoriously, but quickly met her next opponents. Before her stood Dragon and Jet, who had just finished off Kiera.

"You can't rely on anyone these days," muttered Lexie under her breath, "if you want something done right, then I guess you have to do it yourself."

The tombstone failed to permanently render Goldilocks unconscious, as she stood to her feet and walked over to join Jet and Dragon.

"What the hell is Goldilocks made of?" muttered Lexie, choosing to start with Dragon.

They blocked and countered each other until Lexie performed a triple roundhouse kick with the same leg. While the girl staggered backwards, Goldilocks grabbed Lexie from the rear. Jet tried to seize her opportunity and walked in. Lexie, who was still trapped in Goldilocks's arms, managed to jump and kicked both legs out hard in front of her and into the other girl's face. Jet flew across the canvas and over the top rope. Now there were just two girls left in the match.

Goldilocks threw Lexie hard, she flew across the ring. She glided to a stop on the top rope just as Dragon came in close. Lexie performed a back somersault off the ropes and landed behind Dragon. She turned around to face Lexie just as Lexie jumped and performed a flying side kick, knocking her out of the ring. Only one girl left, the Russian champion. It was a showdown. They stood there staring towards each other, trying to intimidate the other person. Then Lexie conjured up a plan to hypnotise the pretty Russian girl. She stared deeply into her big green eyes and blinked, but nothing happened so Lexie blinked once more.

"Have I lost my powers or is Goldilocks not human?" thought Lexie.

Goldilocks wondered in closer, stood before her and said,

"Having trouble making a telepathic connection?"

Lexie accepted that she was unable to compel her to do her biddings. She glanced down at her waist and there was no sign of a magical belt.

"What are you?"

"I'm a replicator," replied Goldilocks.

For a few seconds they stared directly into each other's faces. The cameras around the arena slowly began to zoom in on them. High on one side of the ring was a huge TV screen, which was projecting what was happening in the main ring. Then the scene changed and it was now showing the gigantic face of… Dr Dre.

Chapter 9

There was the sound of murmuring heard all around the Bruno arena. Spectators now became concerned about who had interrupted their entertainment. Violet and Tamir sat bolt upright in their seats and glared at the screen.

"Is that who I think it is?" Tamir asked.

"I told you we weren't imagining him," replied Violet.

Lexie and Goldilocks both stared towards the large screen. There was the sound of laughter before Dr Dre began to speak.

"I don't know how you girls managed to save the HS3 train from crashing, so I will now punish you for trying to make a fool of me. This is my world and I have eyes on you, wherever you go. You will fight Goldilocks and you will lose the match. Then you will finally hand over your belt. If not, I have already wired this arena with several plastic explosives. If Violet or Tamir try to leave their seats, then everyone dies. The explosives are set to explode in five minutes. You have five minutes to hand over your belt or everybody in this arena dies. Have I got your attention now?"

The murmuring began to get louder as people began to panic.

"We can't just sit here and do nothing," said Tamir.

"Let's see if Lexie can work out how to get out of this tricky situation," gestured Violet.

"Surely you can come up with a strategy, since you use 70% of your brain," commented Tamir.

"Lexie's like an oracle," responded Violet.

Dr Dre proceeded saying, "All the entrances have been secured, so nobody leaves. You cannot win, so fight without the use of your force field. Goldilocks will humiliate you in front of hundreds of spectators, unless you hand over your belt so that we can discover the source of your powers."

Lexie stood in silence, contemplating her next move.

"People are beginning to panic," whispered Tamir.

"Lexie will think of a plan." returned Violet softly.

"You have five minutes. Let the fight begin," ordered Dr Dre.

Out of nowhere, Goldilocks gave Lexie a hard side kick to her torso and she flew across the canvas. Several spectators screamed in fear for this teenager's life. Lexie returned to her feet lazily. They exchanged blows and Lexie went down. Dr Dre cackled with excitement. His face now took up a small corner of the gigantic screen, which was now zooming in on the fight. Goldilocks picked Lexie up by her hair as she screamed in pain. All she had to do was turn back on her invisible force field and the pain would go away, but at the expense of killing hundreds of spectators. No, Lexie had to endure the physical torture until she could work out a strategy to save everyone. Spectators along with Violet and Tamir gasped, watching Lexie being overpowered by Goldilocks. Two minutes had lapsed before Lexie managed to send a message to Violet and Tamir telepathically.

"Any ideas yet girls?"

"We were hoping that you would come up with a plan to get everyone out of here unharmed."

"Err, you want me to think of a plan in the middle of being battered around this ring?"

"Multitask," replied Violet sarcastically.

Lexie grunted as she was hit in the face with a hard right hook, which knocked her down to the canvas with a thud.

"Dr Dre said that you can't get out of your seats, but he didn't say you couldn't use your abilities to track where all the explosives have been placed."

Violet glanced around the arena.

"I'm not picking anything up visually," said Violet.

Lexie blocked a kick that was directed towards her nose and grappled Goldilocks to the canvas. They lay there wrestling each other, while Lexie attempted to formulate another plan.

"I'll see if I can home into the bombs digital frequency that's connected to the timer."

"Will you be able to concentrate at the same time of getting your head smashed in?" thought Tamir compassionately.

"Yes, no problem," said Lexie sarcastically just as Goldilocks bounced her head off the canvas several times.

They lay there wrestling, while Lexie attempted to focus on locating the bombs using her new ability. She went into surveillance mode and scanned the arena.

"I've managed to locate the explosives."

"How many are there?" asked Violet.

"Four."

"That's too many," thought Tamia, "we could get to two, but if Dr Dre sees us shimmer in our seats, he will detonate the other two."

"We are going to need help," thought Violet.

"I could try and compel Kiera and Rebecca again using mind control."

"You have less than two minutes to disarm the bombs," thought Violet.

"I can do it," Lexie responded.

"Go for it girl," encouraged Tamir.

Goldilocks trapped Lexie's arm on one leg, whilst laying on the canvas. She pulled hard with both arms attempting to break her elbow, using her leg as leverage. Goldilocks had her other leg wrapped around Lexie's throat as she began to choke her. Lexie was unable to speak, but she was able to still use her telekinesis ability. The two girls were still under Lexie's mind control and susceptible to suggestion, so Lexie compelled both Kiera and Rebecca to follow her orders and they went in search of the bombs.

They quickly found the explosives, picked them up as instructed and hurried back towards the ring side. Running out of time, Dr Dre came back on the large screen with a message saying, "You have less than one minute to lose this match and surrender your belt, or I will detonate the bombs."

Goldilocks picked Lexie up by her hair once more and then punched her to her torso several times, knocking the wind out of her. There was now only twenty seconds left and the two girls had not returned to give the bombs to Violet and Tamir, who were sat, unable to move off their seats at the ringside.

"There they are," said Tamir.

"I don't think that they're going to make it," remarked Violet.

The two girls had converged together and were now quickly shuffling through the crowd walking side by side towards the ring.

"Ten seconds left," announced Dr Dre.

Spectators scrambled out of their seats in a frantic rush. The sound of panic was everywhere. They all knew that they were literally seconds away from being blown to smithereens.

"Scrap that, let's try a new plan," relayed Lexie just as Goldilocks picked her up high above her head in preparation to throw her.

"What do you suggest?" asked Violet.

Lexie used her telekinesis to direct Tamir to the girl's bathroom and Violet to the main entrance, to retrieve the missing bombs. It all happened in a flash. With just five seconds left before detonation, both Violet and Tamir Launched out of their seats and vanished. Goldilocks threw Lexie high into the air and she went hurtling towards the top rope. Then to everyone's surprise, Lexie too disappeared. Kiera and Rebecca took one more step towards the ring and the bombs suddenly vanished out of their hands. Lexie managed to retrieve the two bombs and wiz quickly into the upper atmosphere, teleporting at lightning speed. She joined her two sisters as they made a rainbow high in the sky. The bombs safely exploded. They then flew back down. Two of them go back to their seats and Lexie teleports back in the ring behind Goldilocks.

Goldilocks blinked a few times and shook her head in confusion of where her opponent had vanished to. Then she slowly turned around and had a surprise.

Lexie walked towards Goldilocks and said, "My turn," Lexie beckoned.

With that Lexie performed a jump back kick which knocked her clear across the ring. She bounced off the ropes and headed back. They exchanged blows, blocking and striking each other, but

Lexie's reflexes were too quick. This time Goldilocks was down, but not out. The crowd of spectators roared with excitement. Lexie approached and Goldilocks executed a kick to her chest. Lexie too was down, they gazed towards each other with rage.

"And now my full 100%," said Lexie.

They both sprang to their feet and met in the middle of the ring. Lexie punched and kicked at an alarming pace that Goldilocks was unable to keep up with. She decimated her until her face was contorted from the rapid blows. Finally, Lexie screamed, spun around twice, performing a 720 degrees cyclone kick. Goldilocks flew across the ring and landed on the canvas near the ropes.

For a few seconds she lay there as though she was out, but to everyone's surprise she then rolled out of the ring. She reached down under the canvas of the ring to retrieve a weapon. Then she re-emerged with a baseball bat.

"See how you fend against this," threatened Goldilocks.

Spectators gasped in fear.

"That won't save you," commented Lexie while approaching her.

Lexie had her invisible force field fully up. All her wounds had regenerated and healed rapidly. Goldilocks swung hard, but Lexie dodged her every strike. Eventually Lexie blocked and held tightly onto the baseball bat. Goldilocks attempted to break free from her grasp, but Lexie was too strong. Suddenly Goldilocks pressed the base of the bat, which released a long sword from within. Lexie, with her super quick reflexes, somersaulted back a few times before standing firmly to her feet.

They stood peering directly into each other's eyes.

"You're finished, little girl," Goldilocks bellowed confidently.

Lexie wasn't taking any chances. She was worried that Dr Dre may have tampered with the sword, and it might be able to penetrate her force field. She reached into her magical belt to produce a three-section staff. It looks similar to Nunchucks, but with three wooden sticks, held together with two short chains. Lexie swung it around her body a few times and then finished in a strong fighting stance. Goldilocks's eyes widened in surprise before she lunged forwards with a few strikes. Lexie's lightning speed was able to block her every attempt.

"Should we help her?" asked Tamir, directing it towards Violet.

Lexie then performed a strike towards Goldilocks's jaw with one of the amber coloured sticks and knocked her to the canvas.

"Help which one?" responded Violet cheerfully.

Goldilocks looked frightened as she slowly got back to her feet. She came in hard, swinging from left to right. Lexie managed to block her strikes. Then Lexie released her grip from one stick and swung the other. Her three-section staff became much longer, and she was able to knock Goldilocks's sword out of her hand from a distance. The sword landed on the edge of the canvas. Goldilocks fought on but had no chance fighting unarmed against a weapon. Lexie quickly swung the centre stick over Goldilocks's head. When the stick was lowered down behind her ankles, Lexie pulled hard on the two remaining sticks. It swept Goldilocks off her feet and flat on her back. She slowly sat up and turned her head to look over her shoulder towards the sword. Before she could spin her head back to face Lexie, she was hit with another strike which knocked her across the canvas. She landed hard on her back and lay there helpless.

Lexie collapsed her three-section staff and held it in one of her hands. She then slowly walked forwards and stood over her. They looked into each other's eyes for a few seconds, while Goldilocks pondered on her next move. Lexie shook her head and said,

"I advise you to stay down."

Goldilocks was badly damaged. Spectators watched as she slowly transformed into a small replicator. It darted around the canvas ring for a few seconds, with its poisonous antenna, but was unable to catch Lexie. Then it just disappeared.

"I knew she was too pretty to be a human," commented Tamir.

"I thought that Russian girls had dark hair," replied Violet.

There was silence in the arena. Everyone, including Lexie then glanced towards the large screen. Dr Dre's face became enlarged and stared towards Lexie with indignation. He had witnessed another defeat. He pressed his detonator several times, but there was no explosion. For a few seconds, through the deafening silence, you could have heard a pin drop. Then, in an angry tone, Dr Dre said, "You girls have declared war."

Lexie launched high into the air and performing a jumping scissors front kick with aggression, connected with the surveillance camera. It smashed into pieces and Dr Dre's face disappeared from the screen.

Chapter 10

The three girls left the Bruno arena and wandered outside in silence.

"Are you feeling alright?" Tamir asked, breaking the silence and directing her speech towards Lexie.

"Yes."

"You are a little quiet," said Violet.

"My mind keeps drifting back to Red."

"We will find Roxie Red," encouraged Violet.

"I still can't believe that she is still alive somewhere," said Tamir, "I attended her funeral and witnessed her face in the casket moments before she was buried. For five months we have all been under the impression that she was gone, and we all went off to pursue our own journey."

"We need to let the other Rainbow girls know that Red is still alive," said Violet.

"Okay, but I'm not sure they are going to believe that Dr Dre is back," expressed Tamir.

"You saw him for yourself."

"I did."

"So maybe the rest of the Rainbow girls will believe you, rather than believing me who has been missing for months."

Both Tamir and Violet, stopped and turned to face Lexie who was still too quiet.

"Who do you think we should call first?" Tamir asked trying to include her into the decisions.

"Helen," replied Lexie.

"Why her?" asked Violet.

"I am worried, because we haven't heard from her since she went back to spy on your mum," replied Lexie.

"Do you really think that something has happened to Helen?" Tamir asked.

"I've got a feeling something is wrong, and she is hurt," said Lexie.

"Helen can take care of herself," said Violet.

"I know," said Lexie, "but I still have a gut feeling that she is in trouble."

"I will call Helen right now," said Violet.

"And I will call Gloria," said Tamir.

They both glanced towards their mobiles in their left palm. Different colours flashed across their screens. Finally, there was just a red flashing light.

This time Lexie broke the silence and said,

"Any luck?"

"No answer from Gloria," said Tamir.

"There is no signal with Helen's mobile," answered Violet.

"Now are you worried?" said Lexie in a concerned tone.

"Let me try India," said Tamir.

A few more seconds passed.

"Any luck?" Lexie asked.

Tamir shook her head in disappointment.

"What the hell is going on?" asked Violet.

"Let me try and see if I can pick up a signal," said Lexie.

"How?" asked Tamir.

"It's a new ability she has developed."

Tamir tried to call Gloria once again and the line went dead.

"I am unable to sense anything," said Lexie.

"What about Helen?" asked Violet while dialling.

"Nothing," said Lexie, "maybe someone is blocking their signals."

"Where did Gloria say she was going after Red's funeral?" Violet asked.

"China," replied Tamir.

"You do realise how huge China is," commented Violet, "could you be more specific?"

"Her parent's house in Shanghai."

"I guess we are going to Shanghai to see if we can Pick up any trails," said Lexie.

"I'm still worried about Helen," said Violet.

"Why don't you two girls go and find Gloria and I will go and check up on Helen back at your mum's house," suggested Tamir.

They all walked towards a quiet corner, preparing to teleport to their agreed destinations.

In a split second, Lexie and Violet emerged outside Gloria's family home in Shanghai, while Tamir appeared outside Violet's. Tamir glanced around to see if she could see any visual clues to

Helen's disappearance. Wendy's hover car was parked close by, so she knocked the door. It opened and stood before her was Wendy, Violet's mum.

"Hi," said Tamir cheerfully.

"Good heavens, you gave me a fright," responded Wendy.

"How are you?"

"I am fine," replied Wendy, "I haven't seen you since you left after Roxie Red's funeral."

"We struggled to accept her death and all went our separate ways."

"Come in, come in," Wendy beckoned.

Tamir took a seat inside and quickly scanned the room. Then she listened intently for any sounds of company but concluded that Wendy was home alone.

"So, what brings you back?" asked Wendy.

"I heard that Violet was back in town so wanted to meet her."

"What, you haven't seen her yet?"

"No," Tamir lied.

Wendy looked disapprovingly towards her.

"How did you find out Violet was back?"

"Helen told me and asked to meet her here. Have you seen her?"

Wendy paused in thought before responding.

"Yes, I think that she is upstairs."

"What," said Tamir in surprise, "Helen's here?"

"Yes, I will go and fetch her for you."

Wendy shuffled out of the room, while Tamir wondered to herself how she could have missed sensing Helen when she scanned the house using her superpowers.

A short moment passed; Wendy came back into the room accompanied by Helen.

"You're here, you're okay," bellowed Tamir joyfully.

"Yes, I'm fine," replied Helen coldly.

"Tamir says you planned to meet Violet here," said Wendy while staring directly into Helen's eyes.

"Did we?" asked Helen. Wearing a baffled expression across her face.

"Yes," replied Tamir, "didn't you get the message on your mobile?"

"Oh sorry, my mobile is damaged."

"What, how?"

"I can't remember," replied Helen hesitantly.

Tamir stared at her face. She looked fine, maybe a little vacant, but fine.

After a short while, Wendy decided to invite them both to stay for tea. Now that Tamir had found Helen, she agreed, and Wendy left the room.

"What the hell happened to you," Tamir whispered hastily.

"Nothing."

"Violet asked you to watch her mum and report back."

"Wendy has been kind and she invited me to stay for tea."

"Has she been acting out of character?"

"No, she's great company. She even invited me to stay in her guest room."

"I checked earlier, you were not in this house."

"Wendy called me and asked me to teleport into the guest bedroom."

"Why would she ask you to do that??"

"To meet you," replied Helen with a vacant face.

"Somethings not right," said Tamir, "I'm calling Violet to let her know that I have found you."

Just then, Wendy returned into the room with tea and biscuits.

"Here you go girls," said Wendy, "oh sorry, are you on your phone?"

"Yes," said Tamir, "I'm just letting Violet know that we are here."

Wendy sat down and munched on a biscuit.

After the call, Helen asked Tamir where she had been for five months, but Wendy interrupted their conversation saying,

"So where is Violet?"

"China," Tamir replied.

"Why has she gone there?"

"Umm, to visit some friends I think."

"Which part of China?"

"I can't remember," answered Tamir cleverly.

"Hmmm," thought Wendy.

"You girls drink up your tea and I'll go and get you a little surprise," Wendy said cunningly.

She then hurried out of the room.

A few minutes later, Wendy came back holding a bottle.

"Whatever is that?" asked Tamir.

"Have you finished your tea?"

"Yes," replied Tamir.

"Then would you like to join us in drinking this Authentic Russian Rum?"

"It's really tasty," said Helen.

Tamir glanced towards Helen who was now smiling with glazed eyes as though she was in a trance. Tamir then hesitated before she answered, feeling as though she was being compelled to agree.

"Sure," she replied.

Wendy gave a crooked smile while pouring some liquid into their glasses.

"Now drink up girls."

They took a few sips before Tamir said,

"Is it getting hot in here or is this drink too strong?"

"It's tasty, isn't it?" Wendy asked.

"Yes, yes, it is tasty," answered Tamir.

Wendy laughed.

Tamir felt slightly dizzy. She now felt as though she had lost her will to resist whatever Wendy commanded. Wendy waited a few more seconds to make sure that she was susceptible to suggestion and then the real questions began.

"So where have you been for five months?"

"I've been in Vegas running the Bruno foundation."

"How were you able to defuse those four explosives in the arena?"

"Violet and I found one each and Lexie disposed of the other two."

"But how were you able to learn the locations of the bombs so quickly?"

Tamir paused, trying her hardest not to give away any secrets, but she felt compelled to continue answering.

"Lexie has a new power."

"And what is Lexie's new power?"

"She can sense digital signals."

"That's incredible," muttered Wendy, "are you telling me that she can pick up on mobile phone frequencies?"

"Yes."

"Then, put this in your left palm."

Wendy reached into her handbag and revealed a small blue crystal. She passed it over to Tamir who closed her left palm. An electrical current passed through her body and then her hand immediately began to vibrate.

"What was that?"

"You could say that your mobile service has now been disconnected," Wendy responded.

"What?" said Tamir, looking slightly confused.

There was a short moment of silence before Wendy said,

"I want you both to laugh."

Helen and Tamir began to giggle hysterically and then Wendy joined in.

Moments later, Wendy commanded them to stop laughing and then continued with her interrogation.

"So, where in China has Violet gone?"

"Shanghai," replied Tamir.

"Thank you. Now that wasn't so difficult, was it?"

"No."

"What did Violet go to Shanghai for??"

"To find Gloria."

"Why does she need Gloria?"

"To help her locate Roxie Red and Dr Dre."

"I thought that Red was dead and buried?"

"Violet scanned the grave and the coffin was discovered to be empty."

Wendy then stood up abruptly and said,

"We are wasting valuable time. Do you know the secret of Red's powers that gives her the ability to shoot lasers from her eyes?"

"Her magical belt," answered Tamir.

Wendy growled with frustration, knowing that she had already examined Red's belt with no success.

"Stand up Tamir and pass me your belt," Wendy demanded.

The tough, toned Tamir, stood up, unstrapped her magical leather belt from around her waist and passed it to Wendy without hesitation.

"Now let's prepare a warm welcome for our Rainbow girls," smiled Wendy in triumph.

Chapter 11

I t was Just after 9am the next day. People were starting work in Shanghai. Time seemed to be in control. Lexie and Violet had teleported from Las Vegas at 6pm in the evening. It took them 2 seconds to arrive in Shanghai, yet time says they were into the next day 15 hours later. When you think about it, time zones are quite remarkable and almost magical. The girls observed their surroundings. Tall, beautiful buildings were scattered everywhere. It looked similar to New York, but what was this? Lexie noticed that there were seven churches, a hospital and the Police station all lined up besides each other.

"How strange to arrange their buildings the same as Los Angeles."

"I wonder why?" replied Violet as they walked on.

They came across a large park which was full of people all lined up neatly in rows.

"What are they all doing?" Lexie asked.

"It is traditional for people to spare a few minutes before work to Prepare their body mentally and spiritually by taking part in Tai Chi."

"How cool and calmed they all look and how old."

"Tai Chi is said to lengthen life."

"I sense that Gloria's parents are among the people meditating."

"How would you know that?" Violet asked, still amazed with Lexie's growing abilities.

"There they are," said Lexie pointing to two people in the crowd, "we will join in with the Tai Chi until they finish."

They moved their arms slowly up and down in front of their body. On the way up, they breathed in through their nose, leading with their wrists. On the way down, they slowly breathed their air out through their mouths. It was all done slowly and gracefully.

After half an hour, Gloria's parents began to walk by and Then Gloria's mother locked eyes on Lexie as though she recognised her.

"Hi there, you are Violet's mum Wendy, yes?"

"Umm, no, not quite," replied Lexie in Cantonese.

"You speak Chinese?" Gloria's mum asked.

"I just learnt it," answered Lexie proudly.

"I am Wendy's daughter Violet," added Violet to the conversation.

"You have grown since we last saw you," said Gloria's mum Si-Wei Lee.

"Why does Lexie look just like your mum?" Gloria's dad Wai Lee asked.

"Strong genes, I guess," Violet replied with a slight giggle.

"What brings you girls to China?" Mr Lee asked.

"We are hoping that Gloria can help us find Roxie Red," answered Violet.

"You know Red passed away a few months ago," declared Si-Wei.

"We have just learnt that Red is still alive," responded Violet.

Gloria's parents glanced around nervously and then said,

"Shhh, we cannot talk here. You girls will join us in our home."

During their journey, Violet's mobile rang. It was Tamir confirming that she had successfully found Helen!

It was a beautiful house, with a large, decorated garden. They sat outside drinking tea.

"I can't help but notice that the city was not that busy," said Violet.

"Shanghai has mysteriously become deserted over the last few months," declared Mr Lee, "I would say that about one third of the population has disappeared."

"Same as Los Angeles," exclaimed Violet.

"There have been rumours," whispered Mr Lee glancing around nervously for anyone that could be listening in.

"What kind of rumours?" Violet asked softly.

"They say when you go to hospital, then you never come out," answered Mr Lee.

"Why would you think that?" Lexie asked.

"Chinese people live a long life, but when they turn one hundred, they are summoned by the Government to a hospital appointment," replied Mr Lee.

"But they never return," added Si-Wei.

Lexie and Violet looked with widened eyes.

"What do you think is happening to them?" Lexie asked with growing concern.

"Nobody knows," replied Si-Wei.

They sat around admiring the oriental garden. After a while Lexie asked,

"Why are there seven churches?"

"The Government has said that we are only allowed seven religions, two of the churches are Temples," said Mr Lee.

"That's the same as America," said Violet.

"How strange," said Lexie, "so the Government is controlling everyone."

"That's why grandma is afraid to go to hospital," said Mr Lee.

"What's wrong with your grandmother?" Violet asked.

"Gloria's Grandma is getting very old and is struggling to walk," replied Mr Lee.

"So how do you know Red is still alive?" Si-Wei asked.

"I used my special abilities and scanned her grave, which turned out to be empty," said Violet.

"How can Gloria help you girls?" Si-Wei asked.

"We are hoping that she will give us some clues on what actually happened."

Then Gloria's dad said in a reassuring tone,

"Maybe Gloria can help you."

"How?" asked Violet.

"After Red died, your mum Wendy came to visit and had Red's belt with her," replied Mr Lee.

"What," screamed Lexie uncontrollably.

"Shhh," whispered Si-Wei.

"Are you sure?" asked Violet.

"Yes," answered Mr Lee, "she brought it to my university to be examined."

"What is so special about your university?" asked Lexie.

"Shanghai University has the top science department, equal to that of UCLA or MIT," answered Mr Lee.

"Maybe they were just trying to find out how she died," defended Violet.

"I assure you they were trying to unlock its powers," replied Mr Lee, "because I was part of the team of Scientists running tests."

There was silence. Only the sound of birds chirping in the trees could be heard.

Lexie eventually broke the silence and said,

"I am getting a negative vibe from your mum and that's not easy to accept since she is stunning and looks just like me."

"Tamir called my mobile earlier saying everything was fine and that she found Helen safe and sound," replied Violet.

"Sorry but I still don't trust her," Lexie responded.

"I'll call Tamir now and you can speak to her," said Violet dialling her number telepathically.

Lexie listened in using her telekinesis, but then said,

"The dialling tone has gone dead,"

"I don't understand," said Violet, "I just spoke to her not long ago."

"Somethings wrong with your mum," concluded Lexie.

"How is your dad, Violet?" asked Mr Lee.

"He's in a Psychiatric institute."

"I don't understand?"

"He had a psychotic break."

"I spoke to him just before Red passed away and he seemed full of energy and ideas."

"My mum says he missed me being away from him for over five months."

"There must be more that contributed to his diagnosis," implied Mr Lee.

"Not according to my mum," said Violet.

"Violet's dad told us that Red was still alive," said Lexie.

"Maybe he knows what happened to Red, because he was really excited about discovering new features for her belt," said Mr Lee, "in fact, I'm sure he said there is a copy of Red's belt hanging up in the Science Museum."

"What new features?" asked Lexie.

"I don't know, but he also described another belt with enhanced features and appearance to that belt you are wearing."

They all glanced down towards the golden belt around Lexie's waist, which had colourful diamond studded crystals arranged in a rainbow.

"Didn't you ask Red to bring a belt for me?" Lexie directed towards Violet.

"Yes, she collected it from Francisco just before travelling back in time to save you."

"So maybe Red and your dad Francisco are the only two people that knows the secret of the new belts and that's why they are both missing," said Lexie.

"My dad is not missing, he's locked away."

"They have kept him alive to try and get the-"

"What! What?" Violet asked impatiently.

"I've got it," concluded Lexie, "your dad has been the key to everything the whole time,"

"What do you mean?" asked Violet enquiringly.

"Dr Dre studied and examined Red's belt to discover its secret and failed, so he is keeping your dad alive until he finally gives him the secret to unlock the powers to Red's belt, so that means your mum is working with Dr Dre."

Nobody spoke for a moment. They just kept sipping their Chinese tea.

"What has any of that got to do with churches, hospitals and people going missing?" asked Violet.

"We haven't heard anything from Dr Dre for months, are you sure he is still alive?" Mr Lee asked.

"We need more proof before going back to America to visit your dad," said Lexie.

"What do you suggest?" asked Si-Wei.

"We will wait for Gloria to get back and then we will visit the hospital to find out what is really going on in there," replied Lexie.

"We do not know when Gloria will return from work," said Si-Wei.

"Who does she work for?" asked Violet.

"The Government," answered Mr Lee.

"I think that we are going to need more help," said Violet, "Maybe we should call the Chinese army in as backup, I mean, your army is huge, two million I believe."

"Not anymore," said Mr Lee, "the army was dismantled months ago."

"Who ordered that?" asked Lexie.

"The President," replied Mr Lee.

"Why?" asked Violet.

"He has dissolved the army in every Country and ordered the disposal of all nuclear warfare."

"Our President of America wouldn't allow that act of communism," expressed Lexie.

"There is only one President, and he rules the world," replied Mr Lee.

They all turned their heads and looked hard towards Gloria's dad. Gloria's mum was sat to the right of him and turned her head to peer over her left shoulder. Just then, Lexie zoomed into her face and saw the mark on her right side.

"What is that on the right side of your head?"

"It is a tracker," Si-Wei replied calmly.

"Why do you have it?"

"It is a GPS that everybody has, including me," said Mr Lee, turning his head to reveal his mark.

"Looks like the Government is finally controlling everybody," remarked Lexie.

"It is a good thing," defended Mr Lee.

"What could be classed as good by controlling someone else?" asked Lexie.

"The mark on the side of our head contains a microchip that has 7G technology. We can enter a shop, pick up an item and walk out like a shoplifter. The GPS automatically sends details to our bank account, No more shoplifting and no more criminals."

"Yeah but," stuttered Lexie, "then they can track you wherever you go and that's an invasion of privacy."

"There are no criminals anymore and people can't go missing, because someone in authority always knows where you are using their clever GPS tracker," replied Mr Lee.

Both Gloria's parents smiled joyfully.

"You guys are brainwashed," concluded Lexie.

After a few moments Violet changed the subject and said,

"We need to visit your hospital to see what is going on."

"I don't think that you will get very far," commented Si-Wei.

"Why not," responded Violet, "we both speak fluent Cantonese."

"I can even speak Mandarin," added Lexie.

"Yes, but you do not look Chinese," replied Si-Wei.

"I am a shape shifter so I can change to look like you, or I could go as Grandma to her appointment," suggested Violet.

"How can you do this?" Mr Lee asked, becoming curious.

"Have you got a picture of Gloria's grandma?" Violet asked.

Si-Wei reached into her tiny bag and produced a photo. Within seconds, Violet began her metaphysical transformation.

"That's incredible," bellowed Mr Lee.

"You look just like Grandma," said Si-Wei with a pleasant smile.

They all turned towards Lexie.

"And you, who would you go as?" asked Mr Lee.

Lexie glanced at Violet or should I say Grandma for assistance.

"She could go as you."

Within seconds there stood two versions of Gloria's mum Si-Wei.

"Wow," said Mr Lee, "you look like my wife."

"You look good in that dress," commented Violet.

"You look good too, grandma," replied Lexie.

They all stood giggling cheerfully.

A plan was formulated, they all prepared to leave Gloria's mum behind, while they agreed that Mr Lee would drive them to the hospital in his Hover-car. They both slightly bowed their heads to Gloria's real mum to show respect.

"Are you ready ladies?" asked Mr Lee proudly.

Violet extended her arm for assistance.

"What about helping me, your wife?" asked Lexie.

"Grandma needs more help, remember dear!" replied Mr Lee teasingly.

Violet smiled with her usual cheeky smile, and they were off, gliding through the sky in his Hover-car.

Chapter 12

It took about half an hour before they arrived in the parking area of the hospital. They entered the reception area, queuing up before signing Grandma in for HER check-up. The receptionist sent them into a separate waiting room. It was large with many seats full of patients to be seen. Lexie sat down and went into telepathy mode with Violet who QUICKLY responded with,

"Time to do your thing, daughter."

Lexie went into surveillance mode scanning the entire hospital grounds diligently.

"I am hearing some strange sounds."

"Like what?"

"Muffled screaming and yelling. It sounds like many people shouting different things, all at the same time."

"Do they sound like they are in distress?"

"Yes."

One by one patients were called. Finally it was Violet's turn. Gloria's dad assisted her out of her chair.

"Are you okay Grandma?" Mr Lee asked.

"Violet nodded her head and grunted, while sending Lexie messages using telekinesis SAYING,

"What do you suggest?"

"You go into your appointment, I will head to the girl's bathroom before locating the sounds of distress."

"Sounds like a plan."

"Good luck Grandma!" Lexie jokes.

They both bowed and smiled towards each other, then headed down different corridors.

Doctor Lopan asked many questions Inside the room. Violet admitted that she was having some problems with her knee and was in a lot of pain. The Doctor quickly advised her to stay overnight for further tests. Gloria's dad refused and the Doctor soon became indignant.

"It is my Grandma so why can't I take her back home?"

"She is getting on in age and is no good walking and living in that amount of pain," replied Doctor Lopan.

"She doesn't mind living with that pain. Can't you just prescribe her some painkillers?"

"We do not prescribe painkillers to anyone over the age of ninety."

"Why not?"

"They would be too much of a strain on our economy."

"Then I will just take her back home and deal with her myself."

"I am sorry, but I cannot allow that," replied the Doctor sternly.

"She is my mother, and I can do what I like," returned Mr Lee.

Meanwhile, Lexie traced most of the noise to one room. She persuaded her way past nurses and assistants... with her charm, Of course! She turned the handle of the door and slowly walked in.

Before her were several large cells with steel bars. It was horrifying to see frail elderly people yelling frantically for help.

"Oh my God," cried Lexie while running in.

"Help us, please," someone begged.

"How long have you been here?" Lexie asked.

"Several days," they answered with tears dripping from their swollen eyes.

"What are they planning to do with you all?"

"We are all due for termination."

"Define termination?"

"Mass execution."

Violet had enough of playing helpless Grandma, so waited for her opportunity to use her mind control. Doctor Lopan turned to face her and let her know that she had no choice but to stay overnight in hospital. She looked at him with a fixed gaze and blinked. He stared into her big blue eyes, but nothing happened.

"He's not wearing sunglasses so why didn't that work," thought Violet, "unless he's a replicator."

Violet jumped out of her seat but fell to the floor clumsily.

"Are you alright Grandma?" asked Mr Lee while stooping down to help her back to her feet.

"I forgot who I was for a second," replied Violet.

"Let's leave this hospital," said Mr Lee.

"You can't leave," ordered Doctor Lopan.

"I know that you are not human and that you are a replicator," bellowed Grandma.

"Very clever Grandma," said Doctor Lopan just as his white coat slowly changed into his combat uniform.

"I've got a surprise for you too," said Grandma while slowly transforming back to Violet.

"How good is your Kung-Fu?" asked Mr Lee.

Doctor Lopen's eyes widened. Lexie lunged forwards performing some strikes. The Doctor blocked and countered with a few strikes of his own. They punched and kicked each other, but Violet's reflexes were too quick for him, she soon knocked him down. Mr Lee stood back and watched as the Doctor's countenance changed into a small replicator. It headed to try and inject Mr Lee with its poisonous antenna, but Violet managed to manoeuvre him out of harm's way. The replicator darted around the room frantically trying to inject them once more. Violet quickly headed over to a filing cabinet, picked it up and dropped it onto its back. The replicator was crushed and out of action.

"Case closed and filed away," said Violet, shutting a drawer that had managed to open from the sudden impact.

They headed over to the door and opened it quickly.

"Let's get out of here," said Mr Lee in a frantic rush.

Before them stood several Shanghai Police Officers with guns pointed towards them.

"Freeze," a commanding Officer yelled.

"I think that we are going to need help from Lexie," said Violet while making a psychic connection using her telekinesis.

Violet heard Lexie respond and say,

"I'm afraid I have my own fight here."

"What has happened?"

"I discovered what the hospitals are doing with patients."

"Is it nice?"

"No, it's not nice!"

"We are just about to be arrested… again. Can you get here?"

"No, I have to work out how to release over fifty elderly hostages safely before they are executed."

"So are you saying you need my help?"

"Yep."

Two Officers approached Violet and Mr Lee and prepared to put them in handcuffs.

"I hope you don't suffer from motion sickness," said Violet.

"Why?" asked Mr Lee nervously.

Violet's mobile in her left palm began to flash. She had already sent a message requesting teleportation. Just as the Officers were about to fasten the handcuffs, both Violet and Mr Lee disappeared. He saw as the scene before him melted away and then suddenly looked familiar. Violet had teleported them both back into his Hover-car.

"Wow, magic," said Mr Lee amazed.

"You need to stay here, while I go back in and assist Lexie."

"Okay, okay," replied Mr Lee in haste.

"If I am not back in five minutes, just leave."

With that, Violet vanished.

She reappeared in a room to see Lexie, who was still dressed as Gloria's mum, fighting three Police Officers. Lexie resorted to mostly using her arms during her battle. She had already discovered that she could only kick as high as their knees, because she was still wearing a tight long dress.

"You took your time coming to help," said Lexie knocking one down with a right hook.

"I'm here now, brown cow," replied Violet, attempting to rhyme with humour.

Just then an Officer tried to kick Lexie low. She performed a low palm-heel block in lady horse stance and executed a one-inch Wing-Chun punch at the same time, knocking him clear across the room.

"How rude," said Lexie brushing back her hair.

Violet performed a jump reverse heel kick on the third Officer, they were all down and out.

"So how are things?" asked Violet calmly.

"Just fine," Lexie joked.

Violet turned to face the elderly people still locked in the cells and said,

"How are we supposed to remove so many people without being seen?"

"I'm thinking," replied Lexie.

The sound of footsteps could be heard outside the room. Many of the elderly people were still yelling and crying fearfully for their lives.

"We can't keep them safe from here," said Violet, "let's go outside the door and block the entrance."

Lexie turned to face the captives and said,

"We will be back in to help you."

They quickly ran outside the door, shut it and stood in front.

"Communicate in telepathy mode until you find a way of saving everybody," said Violet.

"How good is your Kung-Fu?" said Lexie, seeing a mass of Police Officers before them.

Gunfire commenced. The bullets hit them, but their force-fields repelled the shots.

"How many are there?" thought Violet.

"I count about eighteen Police Officers."

"Any ideas yet?"

"There's no way we can safely walk out of this hospital with them all."

"So then we fly," answered Violet.

"I need to find somewhere safe close by so I could remove each of the fifty captives," suggested Lexie.

"Well, you need to hurry, because Gloria's dad is waiting in his Hover-car for us, but will leave in less than three minutes."

They both punched and kicked, knocking down several Officers. Their lightning speed overpowered a few more.

"What about the seven churches next door?" thought Lexie.

"Do you think that you could persuade a priest to keep them safe?"

"I'm sure they will say yes if I ask them nicely," Lexie joked knowing that she would probably have to use mind control.

"Go swiftly I can manage these twelve," returned Violet confidently.

Lexie teleported into one of the Temples next door. It was big enough to fit them all, she just needed to make sure that the Priest agreed to hide them. There were just a few elderly people praying. A Priest approached and spoke.

"Why are you here so early?"

"I have about fifty elderly people outside that need hiding away from the Police or else they will be terminated."

"You mean they were due for termination by the hospital?"

"Yes."

"We would be delighted to hide them and keep them safe."

"Why are you so kind without me having to-"

"That's what our churches and Temples do," the Priest interjected, "people come here to seek protection from God and that is exactly what we do. We even disable the GPS in their head."

"How can you do that?"

"We anoint their heads with Holy oil."

"And that's it?" asked Lexie.

"Yes, nothing is impossible with God, you just need to have faith and believe."

Lexie bowed to show a sign of respect and said,

"Please don't have a heart attack, but I will be back in a flash."

The Priest blinked and she was gone.

There was the sound of a timer on a detonator that was beginning to go faster. Hostages screamed with panic. Suddenly there was the sound of laughter coming from a CCTV just before a voice said,

"The bomb will go off in less than one minute. Nobody will save you all."

Lexie appeared beside Violet, knocking out an Officer as she glided to a stop.

"I'm back."

"You took your time."

"I went as fast as I could."

"Any luck?"

"Yes, a Priest is waiting to help the hostages."

"That's great, you help them and I will stay here and finish the last four off."

Lexie teleported inside the room and was met with a strange sound.

"What's that noise?"

"A man on the surveillance camera says it is a bomb," screamed several people hysterically.

"Dr Dre," muttered Lexie, "did he say how long you have before detonation?"

"Less than a minute!"

Lexie wasted no more time. She began her extraction at lightning speed. One by one people disappeared from the prison cells and reappeared in the Temple. Lexie sent a message telepathically to Violet saying,

"Finish them off quickly and meet me in the Temple, because there is a bomb in the cells about to detonate."

"What, a BOMB!" yelled Violet just as she threw an Officer over her shoulder.

Hostages kept disappearing from the prison cells at a rate of-one a second, two a second, three a second and four. Lexie sped up until there were no more. Violet vanished just as the bomb detonated with a loud BANG! She re-emerged in the Temple to see Lexie standing there in the midst of a crowd of cheerful elderly people, all happy to be alive.

Violet glanced around the now full Temple and said,

"Did you manage to save everyone?"

"Yes, everybody is present and accounted for," replied Lexie with a triumphant smile.

"How? Surely you can't be that fast."

The Priest smiled towards Lexie as she said,

"I guess, with God, nothing is impossible."

Gloria's dad prepared to leave. He started up his engine and slightly lifted off. Then to his surprise, Violet and Lexie, who was still dressed as his wife, appeared out of thin air.

"You girls made it."

"Didn't you have faith in our abilities?" asked Lexie.

"Yes dear," replied Mr Lee.

They smiled towards each other.

"Are you sure those hostages are safe?" asked Violet.

"Yes, apparently that's what all the seven churches do. They are there to save people and protect them from evil," replied Lexie.

"So, we need to encourage people to go to church for divine protection?" asked Violet.

"Yes, and we need to pass on that positive message around the World," answered Lexie.

"So where to next?" asked Mr Lee.

"Your home," answered Violet.

"What about the Museum?" asked Mr Lee.

"What Museum?" asked Violet.

"We are just passing it and I thought that you girls would like to examine Red's belt," commented Mr Lee.

"We need to get you back and then return to America to check on my dad," said Violet.

"Don't you think we should check out Roxie Red's belt first?" asked Lexie.

"No, it's just a copy," answered Violet.

"Supposing it's not a copy!" Lexie commented.

Violet turned her head sharply to face her.

"What are you saying?" Violet asked with interest.

"When I touched your dad and had a flashback, Red was not wearing her belt."

"The belt in the science museum could be the real belt," suggested Mr Lee.

"I guess we are heading to the Museum then," agreed Violet.

Chapter 13

They glided through the sky in Gloria's dad's Hover-car. In just a few minutes they were touching down in the car park of the Shanghai Science and Technology Museum.

"Let's go then ladies," said Mr Lee proudly.

"Umm, I think that it would be safer if you stay here out of danger," advised Violet.

"You two girls will look a little out of place here in Shanghai," remarked Mr Lee.

"Why, I'm still dressed as your wife and we are both fluent in speaking Chinese," responded Lexie.

Gloria's dad smiled and then said,

"Okay, I will wait here. Red's belt is hanging up in the Alien Artefact section of the Science Museum."

"Alien section!" squealed Lexie.

"Did I not tell you we found traces of Alien phenomenon?" asked Violet.

"I'm scared now, maybe it's safer for me to go back to my world," suggested Lexie.

"Why?" informed Violet, "we found it back in your time."

"Err, what now?" stuttered Lexie in surprise.

"I uploaded the complete database of our library into your brain, why not connect with it and I'm sure you will find out the answers for yourself."

Lexie relaxed her mind and then information came flooding in.

"They found traces of Alien technology back in 1908. There was said to be a meteor landing in Tunguska Siberia east Russia, on June 30th which flattened over 80 million trees. The so-called meteor was about fifty metres wide."

Lexie's eyes widened in surprise.

"How long do you girls want me to wait before I leave you this time?" interjected Mr Lee.

"If we are not back in an hour, just head home," concluded Violet.

With that, the girls left the Hover-car and wandered into the Shanghai Science and Technology Museum.

It was situated in the large park of Pudonj. The Museum is a huge spiral building with five floors topped with a circular roof made of glass. Over a million tourists used to visit every year. The exhibition rooms include an area demonstrating the first earthquake machine, a spectrum of light showing the power of a rainbow and a Science and history exhibition with mythological animals including a red dragon!

"We are not going to have enough time to experience all of the wonders in this museum," said Lexie.

"Let's just find Red's belt and get out of here," returned Violet.

They made their way up to the top floor, passing the earthquake room and the exhibition room containing mythological creatures.

"That's a very large dragon," said Lexie.

"Let's hope it isn't real," responded Violet.

The Alien artefact room was situated behind the spectrum of light exhibition. Queues of people stood around admiring the colourful spectrum. A huge rainbow bowed up high. At the other end of the rainbow was the glass container containing Red's magical belt. Tourists gazed upon its beauty. Both Lexie and Violet slowly made their way to the front and stood before it.

"What do you think then?" asked Violet.

Lexie stared for a few seconds. Then, almost magically, her vision began to zoom into the belt.

"I think that I have just developed a new power," responded Lexie.

"What are you able to do now?" asked Violet.

"I can zoom into objects to see up close."

"Then use it to study the belt in detail."

Lexie zoomed into Red's ruby crystal. Suddenly it began to light up. Lexie was driven to look down at her own belt which too was illuminating brightly. She then glanced towards Violet's belt around her waist and noticed the purple crystal parrot was flashing.

"I think that it is Red's real belt," said Lexie.

"What makes you think that?" asked Violet.

"Look down at your belt and you will see that Red's belt has made a connection, rendering it part of the Rainbow girls."

Violet glanced towards her belt and saw the purple parrot flashing brightly.

They stood among the crowd of tourists for a few seconds before Violet responded saying,

"We can't leave it here."

"I know," said Lexie, "when we find Roxie Red, she is gonna need that belt to restore her abilities."

They stood and pondered their next move.

Lexie glanced around the room. In the distance, she saw another strange shaped crystal in a glass container. Using her new super ability of zooming in, she began to read the label. It confirmed what she had already learnt from having the entire contents of the future electrobase library downloaded into her mind. The crystal was found at the Tunguska crash site in Siberia back in 1908. Apparently, it is only part of a larger crystal.

"That blue crystal over there is from an alien spaceship found in Siberia," said Lexie.

Violet glanced in the direction of the glass container and said,

"What does the label say?"

"It says the crystal contains strange electrical powers."

"Should we take it later?"

Lexie used her 6th sense and said,

"No, something tells me that we should stay well away from it."

"Okay."

"What worries me is that it is only part of a larger crystal that was found."

"So where is the rest?"

"I don't know, but let's hope that it has not fallen into the wrong hands."

After a while, the room containing Roxie Red's magical belt was free from any tourists.

"This is the best time to grab the belt," suggested Violet.

"How?"

"We could smash the glass and teleport out of here before anybody notices."

"It's too noisy, there has to be another way."

"Have you gained any more special abilities?"

Lexie's mind jumbled through a few memories. Then she said,

"Remember back when we were trying to enter your school. I wished that the security's glasses would fly off their faces and it did."

"I thought that it was just good timing. Are you saying you possess the same ability as Red and you can use your telekinesis on objects?"

"There's only one way to find out."

Lexie stared towards Red's belt, which was on a stand behind a thick toughened glass and called out,

"Belt!"

In an instant, Red's belt raised off the stand and magically flew through the toughened glass, landing in Lexie's hand. The girls giggled in excitement. Then Lexie had a psychic premonition. She saw Violet's dad watching his wife strike Roxie Red to the ground.

"What's wrong?" asked Violet.

"I just had another premonition and saw your mum hit Red."

"We need to take this belt and get out of here fast."

Their triumph was cut short. The sensors on the stand had picked up that the belt was missing, and it set off an alarm. The door to the room quickly closed. Lexie hastily lowered Red's belt to her own and it slowly shrunk before disappearing into a hidden chamber within Lexie's belt.

"What's that noise?" Lexie asked as she slowly looked down to the floor.

"I hear nothing," replied Violet.

There was a gentle buzzing noise progressively increasing in volume.

"It's getting louder. Can't you hear it?" asked Lexie.

"Yes, it sounds similar to the noise we heard in the Police Station, come on, let's get out of here," returned Violet.

Both girls prepared to fly off, but there was no movement.

"What's going on?" asked Lexie.

"I can't fly," answered Violet.

"Maybe that noise is some type of electro-magnetic force preventing us from leaving."

"Then we are trapped… again," concluded Violet.

Gloria's dad grew anxious. Several Shanghai Police Officers had flooded the car park and surrounded the entrance to the Science Museum. He had waited over an hour and felt that he just had to leave without the girls. He lifted off and headed towards his home. On the way he noticed that two Police Hover-cars were following him.

"How did I get myself into this mess?" thought Mr Lee.

The Rainbow girls managed to hover a few feet off the ground in preparation to be electrocuted. Then a girl appeared before them with a red dragon on the front of her t-shirt.

"You girls are under arrest."

"Dragon," said Lexie, "didn't I kick your butt back in Las Vegas?"

"I don't know who you are," Dragon responded.

"Violet, if you could transform me, please."

Violet raised her left arm. Her mobile flashed a few colours and Gloria's mum's appearance slowly faded away and transformed back into Lexie.

"Recognise me now?"

"Hand me the belt or you will face my alter ego," warned Dragon.

"Alter ego," mocked Lexie, "what, are you going to change into a dragon or something silly?"

Lexie began to chuckle to herself.

The girl's countenance slowly changed. A huge red dragon now hovered before them, roaring with rage.

"You had to annoy her, didn't you?" said Violet while slowly backing off.

"I didn't know that she could really change into a dragon," yelled Lexie who slowly floated behind Violet.

"What are you doing back there?" Violet asked.

"Hiding behind my big sister," replied Lexie with a nervous smile.

"Well I'm not fighting a dragon by myself," grumbled Violet.

"Shall we just flee?"

"And leave these tourists to the hand of the dragon, no, we will face our fear and defeat the dragon."

"You take the front, I will take the tail," suggested Lexie.

"No way, you take the front," replied Violet.

The dragon lunged forwards towards them both, while snapping its teeth. Violet floated to its left while Lexie whizzed to the right. The dragon didn't know which direction to look in and became confused. It roared loudly and snatched forwards with its paws. The girls had super quick reflexes and dodged every strike. It extended its arms and Lexie began to block and counter with strikes of her own. Violet jumped on its back but couldn't hold on and ended up sliding off.

"Well, that didn't work," gasped Violet.

After a while, the dragon grew tired and began to lash out with its tail. It managed to strike Violet and she tumbled through the air.

"I changed my mind," said Violet, "you can take the tail."

"I've already got the front," replied Lexie, sounding out of breath.

Violet glanced up to see Lexie standing in the dragon's mouth, while preventing it from closing to eat her.

"Okay then," said Violet, "I guess the tail isn't that bad."

"Chair," commanded Lexie.

A chair flew up and landed in one of Lexie's hands. She grabbed firmly to one of its legs and then shoved it into the dragon's mouth. The dragon shook its head from side to side in an attempt to dislodge the chair, but was unsuccessful.

"Way to go girl," said Violet.

"Eat that," bellowed Lexie victoriously.

Then its tail began to curl around Violet's waist and squeezed tightly.

"Me and my big gob," complained Violet.

Lexie flew around to its rear and said,

"It's giving you a hug."

"Help me, you little brat, it's squeezing the life out of me."

"Okay grumpy pants."

Lexie reached into her belt and produced her three-section staff. She swung it around her waist and then proceeded to fight the dragon. She blocked and then hit the dragon in the face, but it had no effect. After swinging it around her body a few times, she flew up to the back of the dragon's neck. Then she whipped one end around the throat and court it with her other hand. Lexie then crossed the two sticks around the back of the dragon's neck. It caused the centre stick to squeeze hard against the front of the neck and it began to choke. The dragon fell hard to the ground with an almighty thud and its tail slowly released its grip on Violet.

"I can't fly fast enough to get out of here," said Violet, "we are still trapped."

"Maybe not," responded Lexie hovering off the floor.

The buzzing sound got louder. Suddenly the dragon court on fire.

"Run," screamed Lexie while grabbing tightly onto Violet's hand and accelerating quickly.

"What the hell," yelled Violet in telepathy mode.

"The floor is electrified again."

Then red, blue and white laser beams appeared. Lexie accelerated even faster to avoid being hit. Their rainbow colours began to get brighter. Lexie's velocity increased so much that their countenance became brilliant white.

"Hold on tight," screamed Lexie.

A whirling sound could be heard as she whizzed around and around the room until her speed was fast enough to break through the toughened glass roof. As they smashed through, a rainbow was produced high in the sky.

One of the Police Hover-cars fired towards Gloria's dad. It hit and he lost control. All his electronics were out, and he plunged towards the ground. Suddenly a rainbow appeared. Lexie had teleported them into his Hover-car.

"We are back," said Lexie boastfully.

"This Hover-car is out of control," responded Gloria's dad.

"Out of the frying pan into the fire; you mean to tell me you teleported us out of one dangerous situation into another one?" yelled Violet.

"Have you any power at all?" asked Lexie.

"No," replied Mr Lee.

"We can't teleport out of here or else it will plunge to the ground and hurt innocent people," advised Violet.

"I guess I'm just gonna have to fly this thing myself," concluded Lexie.

She teleported outside and landed on the roof of the Hover-car.

"What the hell am I doing out here!" bellowed Lexie to herself.

Her hands became fastened to the roof. The amber crystal on her belt flashed brightly as she took over control and began to drive the Hover-car from its roof.

"It's working," said Gloria's dad, "we have levelled out."

Lexie sent a message to Violet in telepathy mode saying,

"I'm gonna head out towards the sea and then I need you to overpower the two Police Hover-cars."

"Message received clearly," replied Violet.

Lexie accelerated and manoeuvred, avoiding blasts from the two Police Hover-cars that were chasing them. In a short moment they were flying over clear water.

"Your turn," echoed Lexie telepathically.

Violet disappeared and entered one of the other Hover- cars. She was met by four men. Battling against all odds she was able to overpower them all. Then she directed the Hover-car to crash into the sea.

"One down and one to go," said Violet back to Lexie telepathically.

Violet vanished and reappeared in the other Police Hover-car. She struggled more with them, because two of them had proton guns. Even though her force-field withstood the blows, she was unable to overcome them before hitting land again.

"How are you getting on?" asked Lexie.

"Just two more guys."

"Too late, you can't take the risk of crashing it on land. Just get back to Gloria's dad."

In the middle of her battle, Violet disappeared and teleported back.

"What now?" asked Violet.

"Ask Gloria's dad how fast this thing goes."

"About 400 miles per hour," he responded.

"Not anymore," said Lexie.

"I think that you should hold on tightly and I hope you are wearing your seatbelt!" advised Violet.

Lexie accelerated to the speed of sound. Now travelling at seven hundred and sixty seven miles per hour, from the front screen of the other Police vehicle, Gloria's dad's Hover-car simply vanished out of sight.

Lexie guided the Hover-car towards Gloria's dad's house. She decelerated and appeared to be just a normal Hover-car, but with a young lady on its roof! They came to a gentle stop, and all vacated the vehicle.

"I can't believe that we are all back safely," said Mr Lee while breathing in clean fresh air.

"Another successful mission," boasted Lexie.

"Thanks for all your help," said Violet, directing it towards Gloria's dad.

"I didn't do anything," said Mr Lee.

"You helped us retrieve Red's belt and now it has given us her location," said Lexie.

"Where has she been held?" asked Mr Lee.

"She's held hostage in the same hospital as my dad," said Violet.

"We are gonna have to leave," said Lexie.

"You can't leave without seeing Gloria," said Mr Lee.

"We will have to resume finding Gloria for another day," said Violet.

Gloria's mum Si-Wei came out to join them.

"Will you stay for something to eat before leaving?"

The girls agreed and entered the house.

It was now just after midnight and the beginning of Friday morning. They had eaten and freshened up and were ready to leave.

"Thanks for all your hospitality. It is getting late so we are gonna have to get back to America," said Violet.

They all stood up and bowed as a sign of respect. The Rainbow girls vanished and then teleported outside Violet's dad's hospital.

Chapter 14

In a flash, they had travelled back in time. They left China at midnight on Thursday and arrived at 9am Thursday morning in America! Although they had taken a split second to reach their destination, time managed to beat them again with the help of the different time zones. The hospital had only just resumed service in the morning, so they wandered in. The crystal on Lexie's enchanted belt began to flash red and amber just as Roxie Red's belt started vibrating.

"My belt has sensed Roxie Red. She is here somewhere in this hospital."

"I need to rescue my dad first."

They used their telekinesis on the receptionist to gain access into the hospital. This time, standing outside Violet's dad's room were two Police Officers with guns prepared for trouble.

"Great," complained Lexie, "are we going to have to fight again?"

"Yes," answered Violet, "unless you have any other bright ideas."

"Teamwork. Are you ready?"

"Born ready," replied Violet.

Lexie shouted,

"Guns."

The weapons lifted out of the Police Officer's hands and landed in Lexie's palm. The Officers turned their heads to face the girls. Lexie then yelled, "Sunglasses."

Their glasses flew off their faces. Violet blinked and immediately made a psychic connection. Then she said,

"Now go to sleep you schmuck."

Both Officers fell to the ground with a thud, fast asleep.

"Now that's fighting without fighting," said Lexie with a cheerful smile.

They walked in and found Francisco rocking in his chair, mumbling incoherently.

"Dad, it's me, Violet."

Her dad stared as though he no longer recognised his daughter.

"What's he saying?" asked Lexie.

"Nonsense."

"He's not in his right mind."

"Come on, help me get him out of this chair."

Lexie took hold of his other arm. She had an immediate psychic premonition and said,

"Your dad definitely saw what happened to Roxie Red. They must have been in the same room for a while, because they were in a room with padded walls of Red."

"Let's take him somewhere safe before rescuing Roxie."

"Like where?"

"We can't take him home."

"What about teleporting him into one of the churches?" suggested Lexie.

"Good idea," Violet replied.

Violet held firmly to her dad, and they all vanished.

Lexie approached the Priest and asked if they could look after Francisco for a few hours.

"Everyone is welcome in church," answered the Priest, "some people come here to pray, others use it as a fortress of solitude. We try to help everyone in need of healing, guidance or protection."

"Do you anoint their head with oil to disable the GPS tracker?" asked Violet.

"Yes."

"What do you know about the mark on their head?"

"It is a cunning way of controlling everybody. The mark is actually a small barcode that connects people to the Government's electrobase."

"But why?"

"So that the Government knows where everybody is at all times. The electrobase is similar to the old database but holds everything on each person, even where they have travelled, pictures and videos."

"Where have all the banks disappeared to?" asked Violet.

"The palm of their right hand!"

"Wait, what?" interjected Lexie.

"There is another small barcode in everybody's right hand that contains bank details."

"I'm sure that I read about that in the Bible," said Lexie.

"Revelations. It is the end times my dear. The people with the mark will be taken away as soon as they turn one hundred years old."

"So that's what they are doing in the hospitals, they are-"

"Terminating people," interjected Violet.

The girls gazed into each other's eyes.

"We need to get out of here and save Roxie Red quickly," concluded Lexie.

With that, they both vanished.

Using teleportation, the girls appeared back outside Violet's dad's room in the hospital. Laying on the floor were the two Officers still fast asleep.

"And stay down," ordered Lexie jokingly.

Violet rolled her eyes and said,

"Which direction to find Red?"

"My belt says Roxie Red is on the 5th floor," informed Lexie.

They walked into the lift and pressed the button to go to the top floor. The doors of the lift opened and they were immediately met with a sea of people, all armed with weapons.

"Shields up," ordered Lexie.

The firing started immediately. Bullets from every direction hurtled towards them. Two guys had sub machine guns and showered them with bullets.

"Those bullets tickle," said Violet.

"GUNS!" yelled Lexie.

The sub machine guns along with other weapons floated over to Lexie. She quickly grabbed them and one by one threw them into the lift. Then she pressed the button for the lift to go back down to the ground floor.

"Now for some unarmed fighting," said Violet just as she lifted into the air and kicked two guys with a double flying side kick. Lexie quickly knocked out three more with a triple reverse heel kick. They continued to block and strike some more. Then Lexie said,

"Maybe it would be quicker if we used our telekinesis on them."

"Go for it," replied Violet.

"Glasses," shouted Lexie.

All the sunglasses flew off their faces. Violet blinked and yelled, "Stop."

Under mind control, they all froze and awaited a command.

"You want to start something boys?" said Lexie victoriously.

"That reminds me of a song," said Violet.

Lexie turned her head towards Violet, smiled and said,

"Let the entertainment begin."

"Sing Starting Something by MJ, please boys!" Violet ordered.

Violet's mobile lit up, vibrated and then played the musical track. The dancing started as they all broke out in song.

You want to be starting something,

You are always starting something,

You want to be starting something,

you're a vegetable.

After a few minutes of watching the performance, Lexie said, "Shouldn't we take this opportunity to rescue Roxie Red uninterrupted?"

"Lead the way," replied Violet.

They walked past the singing and dancing and entered a room. It was a red padded cell dimly lit. There curled up on the floor was… Roxie Red.

"Oh my God, you're still alive," screamed Lexie in hysterics.

Violet rushed over, crouched down and carefully took her into her arms.

"What have they done to you?"

She looked malnourished, almost on the verge of death. Her face had sunken in. She did not have the appearance of the old Roxie Red, who was gorgeous and well-toned.

"You came back for me," said Red weakly.

"You're my sister," replied Violet, "of course I did."

"You're my sister too," said Lexie.

Red turned her head slowly to face Lexie.

"What are you doing in our world?"

"Rescuing you," replied Lexie.

Red managed a slight smile.

"What ever happened to your belt?" asked Violet.

"Your mum took it," whispered Red.

"And now I have it," said Lexie while pulling out a magical belt that began to grow and flash brightly.

"Where did you find it?" asked Red.

"They were doing tests on it and then they left it hanging in the Shanghai Museum."

Lexie handed it over to Violet who quickly placed it around Red's waist. There was a slight delay before the magical powers in the belt began to regenerate Red's cells. Her cheeks puffed out and her arms appeared to grow muscles as she staggered to her feet.

Roxie Red shook her head as though to become more aware of her surroundings.

"I'm still not feeling 100%, maybe you should rescue your mum first."

"My mum is at home and planning something devious. I think that she is a replicator or something, because she is acting out of character."

"Your mum is in the other room, you need to help her quickly," said Red.

"Wait, what!" said Lexie, becoming slightly baffled.

"Your other mum is in the room over there."

They all glanced over to the door that Red was pointing towards. Lexie slowly walked over and entered the room. After a short moment she reappeared holding a woman that resembled her in her arms.

"Mum," Violet screamed.

"She's barely breathing," said Lexie.

"How is this possible?" asked Violet.

"She refused to tell them the secret of your powers, so they tortured her."

"If this is your real mum, then who the hell have we been speaking to in your home?" asked Lexie frantically.

"Let's get them out of here and into somewhere safe," suggested Violet.

"What about the church?" asked Lexie.

"Perfect, let's go," answered Violet.

She held onto Red's arm, they all slowly floated off the ground and then vanished.

After materialising in the church, Lexie handed Wendy over to the Priest to see if he could heal her, while Violet went over to her dad and gave him a big warm hug.

"I've missed you," bellowed Francisco.

"What, you remember me?"

"Yes, I'm all better now."

"I don't understand."

"The Priest anointed my head with sacrificial oil, and it healed me."

"But your psychosis?"

"Sorry dear, but it was all induced. Your mother poisoned me."

"But why?"

"Because I refused to give away the secrets of Roxie Red's belt."

"If she poisoned you, then what of my dog Orion?"

"She poisoned him too."

"Not the dog."

Violet clapped her hand against her mouth in disgust.

"Sorry dear," commented dad.

"She's evil," remarked Violet.

After a few seconds, Lexie walked back over to Violet and said,

"The Priest will look after your mum."

"Oh yeah, dad, this is Lexie," introduced Violet.

"Nice to finally meet you," said Francisco.

"Did Violet tell you how wonderful I am?" said Lexie with humour.

"I already knew who you were before Violet."

"How?" asked Lexie, becoming intrigued.

"I was the one that gave Violet the magical kidney to save you."

"But why me?"

"I knew that our world was on the path of destruction. Someone very beautiful, with special powers gave it to me and instructed me on who to find, so I sent it back with the hope that you would save us all."

"But I'm from the past."

"I thought if you could change the past, then Dr Dre would not be able to destroy our world with nuclear bombs."

"But there are no nuclear weapons here," Lexie informed.

"Somehow Dr Dre has still managed to alter time to his advantage," replied Francisco.

"So, what now?"

"You need to go back in time and make sure that his men don't get away with my formula."

Lexie touched her belt for comfort and then said,

"Did you really design my magical belt?"

"Yes, but the belt isn't the only thing that gives you strength."

"Lexie has had a Dramatic increase of intelligence," interjected Violet.

"It has increased exponentially," added Lexie.

"She's an oracle," said Violet.

"Your powers are now limitless," commented Francisco.

Lexie gave a bright smile. Then Roxie Red came over to join them. She looked revitalised and fresher faced.

"How will we beat Dr Dre when we finally confront him?" asked Red.

"Just remember, his powers reside in his belt," advised Francisco.

"We are going to have to confront your other mum and then find Dr Dre before he terminates any more people," said Lexie.

"I'll come as backup," insisted Red.

"Are you sure that you are up to it?" asked Violet.

"Yeah, let's go and kick that schmucks butt."

"Then let's go," said Violet.

"Good luck girls," said Francisco.

They slowly floated off the ground and then disappeared.

This time they materialised in Violet's home. They called Wendy who was upstairs.

"Maybe you should wait outside until we call for you using our telekinesis," suggested Violet.

"Are you sure?" asked Red.

"I'm sure that I can manage confronting my mum."

"But she's not your mum," remarked Lexie.

Just then, Wendy entered the room.

"Hi girls, why are you not dressed for school?"

"Save it mother, we know that you are an imposter."

"Don't be silly dear, it's me, Wendy."

"We have just come back from the hospital and rescued Roxie and my dad."

"Maybe you are not feeling well dear, let me make you a cup of tea."

"Why, so that you can poison me too?"

"I would never do that."

"Is that why I have been acting strange, did you already try to poison me?"

"Well, I broke her out of your trance," interjected Lexie.

"You girls are wrong, it's me your mum."

"You're an imposter," yelled Violet.

"It's me your mum, pet," insisted Wendy.

"Then where is Roxie Red?" asked Violet.

"Unfortunately, she died," replied Wendy.

Violet called for Red using her telekinesis while saying,

"Then who's this?"

Red materialised into the room. Wendy went quiet as she gazed into her eyes and Roxie Red stared right back.

Red broke the silence first and said,

"We also rescued the real Wendy from the hospital, so who the hell are you?"

Wendy paused, glanced down in disappointment and then said,

"I guess I'm caught."

Her countenance began to change. Her girlish outline disappeared and slowly transformed as someone else.

"Guess who's back?" said the voice.

"No, no, no it can't be," screeched Lexie.

"I am reborn."

"It's Dr Dre," announced Violet.

"Welcome to the next episode!" stated Dr Dre.

Chapter 15

The Rainbow girls stood there, frozen for a few seconds, not sure if what they were seeing was real. Had Dr Dre survived or was it just a hallucination?

"I destroyed you," said Lexie.

"And yet here I stand, reborn. I told you I am immortal," boasted Dr Dre.

"Then we'll destroy you again," said Lexie.

"Maybe we'll lock you in my basement," added Violet.

"Stop your Schoolish pursuits, you will never save the world," returned Dr Dre with a smug smile across his face.

"How did you survive?" asked Lexie.

"When you blew me up, the small particles of my spirit travelled back through the portal and slowly rearranged themselves as me."

The girls' eyes widened as they listened in disappointment.

"Why did you dress up as my mother?"

"Masquerading as your mother was the only way of getting close enough to be able to poison you with cups of tea."

"So now you are admitting trying to poison me?"

"Yeah sure."

"Well, it didn't quite work," said Violet victoriously.

"And it didn't work on me either," added Lexie.

Dr Dre brushed his hand backwards over his bald head and in a disappointing tone said,

"No it didn't."

"I guess my powers have grown too strong for you to affect me," concluded Lexie.

"And now you are going to pay for torturing me," said Red as she lunged forwards with a hook punch to his face which connected.

He staggered backwards to regain his balance and then performed some strikes of his own. Red blocked and countered with a jump spinning heel kick that knocked him down. He was quickly back on his feet fighting for his life. Red was fighting with built up aggression from reliving the memories of been tortured and now it was payback time. She managed to block his strikes and then perform a jump back kick with her heel, knocking him to the ground once more.

"That girl is on fire," said Violet.

"No time for an Alicia Keyes song," commented Lexie.

He growled in frustration and then reached into his magic belt.

"Watch out," screamed Lexie as he produced his proton gun and prepared to fire.

Red's reflex was too quick and hit the gun with lasers from her eyes. The gun melted as he screamed in pain, releasing his grip and dropped it to prevent his fingers from getting more burnt. He stood helpless now facing the three Rainbow girls.

"You're finished," warned Red.

"Give up, you are outnumbered," said Lexie.

Dr Dre slowly scanned the three girls with his eyes and then said,

"Maybe it's time for me to change the odds."

With that he slowly floated off the ground and then disappeared.

Violet ran over to her dog Orion who was sitting quietly in a corner.

"My poor dog, that nasty man tried to poison you. Don't worry, we will find him and punish him for you."

She rubbed his ear and gave him a warm hug. Lexie walked over to Red saying,

"Girl, you were on fire!"

Red smiled and then they all began to laugh. Then Violet said,

"Dr Dre almost looked frightened of you."

"I guess he knew I had some built-up anger to release after he tortured me."

"No, there's more to it," said Lexie, "when you were fighting, I noticed that he kept glancing down at your leather belt."

"Maybe he was afraid of my new ability," said Red.

"What's that?" asked Lexie.

"You will see it soon."

"What about my parents?" asked Violet who was still stroking Orion.

"Red and I will go and retrieve them from the church," replied Lexie.

They slowly floated off the ground and then vanished.

A few minutes later they emerged with Violet's parents. She rose to her feet and gave her parents a warm group hug.

"Mum, dad I missed you."

"We missed you too darling," they responded.

"I am sorry to have put you through that awful ordeal."

"How is it your fault?" asked mum.

"I should have stayed here to look after you instead of travelling back in time."

"I was the one that sent you back in time on a quest to find Lexie to try and save us all," said dad.

"I'm still not sure how I'm supposed to save everyone," interjected Lexie.

"You will find a way to permanently deal with Dr Dre," insisted Francisco.

"He's immortal so will find a way to regenerate," said Lexie.

"You have the power within you, just have faith in your abilities," responded Francisco.

"I guess we better go and find him," said Lexie.

"Not today," interjected Wendy, "you can all stay for dinner and then continue on your quest tomorrow."

Red was the first to agree, after not eating a decent meal for several months.

The next day they all awoke bright and early. Francisco saw them off.

"Now be careful girls, Dr Dre is cunning and will try to find a way to deceive you."

"I'll fry him with my lasers first," said Red.

"Yes," said Lexie, "how did you manage to counteract his poison?"

"He put a bracelet on my wrist to control me. When he left the room, I attempted to break free by aiming my laser directly onto it, but then I guess I slightly missed and ended up burning my wrist. Then I suddenly awoke and was aware of everything."

"That happened to me too," added Violet, "we were fighting in the girl's bathroom at school. You held onto my wrist with your Kung-Fu grip. You gave me a friction burn and then I was suddenly broken free from my trance."

"Maybe that's what's happened to Helen and Tamir," said Lexie, "if they drank Wendy's, I mean the other Wendy's poisonous cup of tea, then they might be under Dr Dre's mind control."

"Oh, that's not good," said Violet.

"Why sound so worried?" asked Lexie.

"Have you seen Tamir angry?" asked Red, "why do you think that we call her Mr T?"

"Lexie can confront her," Violet insisted.

"Why me?" Lexie complained.

"You are the one that will restore world peace," said Francisco.

"You girls can have Tamir, I'm not going near her," responded Lexie.

They chuckled for a while.

"Your powers have been elevated," encouraged Francisco.

"Yeah, dad says your powers are now limitless," said Violet.

"When we retrieved Red's belt from the Museum in Shanghai, there was also a blue crystal there with strange powers," stated Lexie.

"It is of paramount importance that you stay away from the crystal," warned Francisco.

"Why, what will it do?" asked Lexie.

"It can emit an EMP pulse that could hurt you."

"You mean kill me?" corrected Lexie.

Francisco reframed from answering.

"The label says it came from a meteor crash back in 1908 and is part of an alien spaceship," continued Lexie.

"Yes, it did," said Francisco.

"How is that possible?"

"1908 was a leap year, so it must have travelled through the portal."

"Part of the crystal is missing. Have you any idea where the other part is?"

"I had it, but it was stolen after I was poisoned."

"Don't tell me, Dr Dre is now in possession of it."

"Yes."

They all looked at him with a fixed gaze.

Red broke the silence and said, "Maybe we should call the Police for backup."

"Dr Dre has control of the Police," informed Francisco.

"Then we will aim higher and go to the Government," said Lexie.

"I bet he has control over them too," said Violet.

"Then we will aim even higher and go straight to the President," suggested Lexie.

"Let's go," said Violet who was now giving her dad a last hug before departing.

They all smiled at Francisco, levitated off the ground and were gone.

They materialised in the White house and asked to see the President. A security guard got on his phone and relayed a message. They heard him whisper saying,

"The assets have arrived."

"That's what they called us when they took us to the Police Station," said Lexie softly.

"What else did he say?"

"The other voice said to lock it down."

"Shields up," ordered Violet.

"Maybe we should go into telepathy mode," suggested Lexie.

"Do you think that you can use your new power and find out who he was speaking to?"

"He was speaking to someone called senator Reynolds."

"Can you trace where the signal was coming from?" asked Red.

"Yes."

"Cool power," said Red.

"Follow me," instructed Lexie.

The girls vanished from before the security guard and materialised in a dank room. There was no sign of Senator Reynolds, but twenty guys, all with guns, stood before them. They immediately opened fire. Both Red and Lexie called out, "Guns."

Weapons flew into the air and landed in their hands. Violet started kicking and punching guys to the ground. Lexie joined in with some jump kicks, while Red zapped a few guys with her x-ray laser vision. Then she finished them off with kicks.

"Twenty guys down in less than two minutes," boasted Red.

"You cheated," said Violet, "you burnt half of them with your laser and then kicked their butts."

Red smiled victoriously.

"There is another guy over there just sitting there," said Lexie telepathically.

He gazed towards them for a moment and then spoke on his mobile.

"What's he saying?" Violet asked.

"He's speaking to Senator Reynolds and letting him know that the targets survived."

"What did the other person say?" asked Violet.

"Lock it down."

"Can you trace the digital signal again?" asked Red.

"Yep, let's go."

They quickly disappeared and teleported into another room to find three guys pointing crossbows towards them, with several others holding proton guns. Lexie glanced around and concluded that Senator Reynolds had eluded them and disappeared once again.

"Fire," a commanding voice shouted.

Arrows hurtled towards them at the same time as laser beams from the proton guns. Their invisible force field protected them from the blasts, while each of them caught in their hands the arrows in the midst of their flight.

"My turn," said Red, firing lasers from her eyes.

The proton guns just melted. There were screams of terror from the heat emitted. Violet ran forwards and quickly floored two Officers, while Lexie performed a spinning heel kick, and he went down with a thud. The other guys were in no fit state to fight with burnt fingers, so Violet used mind control and compelled them to go to sleep.

Red noticed that there was another security Officer in a corner on his mobile phone.

"What's he saying on the phone?"

"He's speaking to Senator Reynolds who has just ordered to lock it down again," replied Lexie.

"Do you think that they are testing us?" Violet asked.

"Yes, they are prepared for us," answered Lexie, "and are always one step ahead."

"Then we need a strategy," thought Violet telepathically.

"Next time," instructed Red, "we'll deal with the villains, while Lexie uses her new ability to locate Senator Reynolds as soon as he answers the phone."

"Okay," replied Violet.

They teleported into a very large arena. Facing them were rocket launchers and three tanks. Several more security guards stood with other deadly weaponry.

"I changed my mind," said Red, "you can stay here and help us fight."

"Fire!" a commanding voice called out.

"Go, go, go," yelled Violet while taking flight.

There was a sea of gun fire, laser beams and blasts from the three tanks. Lexie glowed brightly from being hit from a proton gun. Her force field held onto the energy for a second. She pointed her arm towards one of the men holding the proton guns and light omitted from her arm. It knocked him clean off his feet. Red then pulled the hood of her red cloak over her head and said,

"It's time for my new power."

Violet turned her head towards Red and said,

"Who do you think you are, little Red riding hood?"

"No," replied Red, "I'm the Big bad wolf!"

For a second, Red looked quite cute with her hood up, but then her countenance slowly changed. Her mouth and nose rapidly grew. She bent forwards and landed on all fours, as both her legs and her arms became huge paws. The red cloak became red hair with the sound of a loud Howell. Before them now stood a giant wolf the size of a huge horse.

"Go get them boy," commanded Lexie.

"Err, she's a girl," corrected Violet sarcastically.

Red could be seen jumping and biting guys. Most of them dropped their weapons, screamed and ran for their lives. There was the sound of a blast. Both Lexie and Violet whizzed through the air to avoid being hit.

"Any ideas?" Violet asked in telepathy mode.

"Yes, stand behind me," replied Lexie.

They glided to the ground and Violet stood behind her little sister for protection.

"Now what?" asked Violet.

"I'll take out the tanks and you finish the three guys off holding the rocket launchers."

Lexie anticipated which guy would fire first. She gazed towards him and called out, "Sunglasses."

He fired just before his glasses flew off his face. Lexie's invisible force field withstood the blast. She began to glow just before pointing an arm towards one of the tanks. She then released the energy from the blast and directed it at the tank. Sparks of fire could be seen before a guy climbed out to safety. Violet swooped in and blinked before saying, "Go to sleep."

Another rocket launcher was fired, and they repeated the exercise. First Lexie contains the blast before redirecting the energy towards another tank. In just a few seconds, all three tanks and guys holding the rocket launchers were out of action.

"Targets eliminated," boasted Lexie.

"Now that's what you call teamwork," responded Violet.

They held an arm in the air and gave each other a high five.

A very large wolf ran towards them. It slowly transformed back into Red, who glided to their side.

"You took your time," said Lexie.

"What!" shouted Red whilst lowering her hood, "you only had three guys to take out each, I had another twenty."

They giggled joyfully.

"They are simply unstoppable," said The President watching from a security camera.

"They haven't been against my personal guards yet," replied Senator Reynolds.

The three girls stood around for a few seconds.

"Did you manage to pinpoint where Senator Reynolds went?" asked Violet.

"Yes, his signal is stable," replied Lexie.

"Let's go get the schmuck," demanded Red.

They teleported into a large room and there standing before them was Senator Reynolds and The President who stared towards them with a fixed gaze.

"No more games," said Lexie, "we've passed all your tests, so it's time to surrender."

"Your combined powers are remarkable," replied Senator Reynolds.

"Mr President, we are the good guys. We are trying to save the world," redirected Lexie.

"Our world is doing just fine without you," said the President, "maybe you should go back to what world you came from."

"Senator Reynolds is feeding you lies," said Violet.

"You girls are villains and should end your quest before you get hurt."

"Senator Reynolds has just been trying to blow us up," said Violet.

"He has been with me all morning."

"We have just followed him through several rooms to get here," said Lexie.

"You girls are mistaken and need to leave."

The Rainbow girls turned their heads to gaze towards the Senator, who's eyes appeared glazed over.

"What have you done to the President?" asked Violet.

The Senator laughed nastily. Lexie used her new power and zoomed into the President's head and there on his right side was the mark of the beast.

"He's brainwashed the President just like everyone else."

Roxie Red's nose began to flare up. She sniffed in search of a stench that was irritating her nose.

"I sense something not nice; I smell... Dr Dre," said Red.

The Senator laughed some more and then said,

"Clever girl."

They stood and watched him go through a metaphysical transformation in plain view, slowly changing back into his human form.

"There," said Lexie, "you can see for yourself, Senator Reynolds is Dr Dre, a crazy criminal."

The President remained silent.

"There are no criminals in my world," said Dr Dre.

"That's because you are the criminal," replied Lexie.

"Mr President, say something," pleaded Violet.

"Don't you girls get it, this is my world and I rule," said Dr Dre.

"The President is in charge," said Violet.

"I am in charge of the President; I rule the world. The President only does what I command."

Lexie stared him down and then said,

"We need to end him."

"You girls are human weapons, imagine if you joined me?"

"We will never join you," remarked Violet.

"Then it will be a waste of abilities seeing you girls defeated today."

"There are three of us and only one of you," said Roxie Red.

Dr Dre cackled with laughter just as they heard a door opening from behind. They turned around to see several people entering the room and walking over to stand in front of Dr Dre.

"Meet my fleet of fighters."

Seven of the girls from the Queen of the ring had entered with Asha-D at the end. Goldilocks was back, with Phoebe the Witch, Dominoah, Kiera, Jet and the twins Rachel and Rebecca.

"I knew I should have let you slap Asha-D again," whispered Violet.

"I have beaten all of those girls before," remarked Lexie.

"Then it's time for you to meet my most trusted bodyguards," boasted Dr Dre confidently.

With a swift breeze, two girls teleported to either side of Dr Dre and there was a moment of silence.

"I guess we finally found Gloria," muttered Lexie in surprise.

Chapter 16

The four missing Rainbow girls stood as bodyguards of Dr Dre. Gloria, India, Helen and Tamir stared towards Lexie, Red and Violet.

"You are grossly outnumbered so give up and join me before you get hurt," ordered Dr Dre with a smug smile across his face.

"Any suggestions?" muttered Lexie softly to both Violet and Roxie Red.

"No, you're the Oracle," whispered Violet.

"Maybe we should communicate in telepathy mode," said Lexie.

"The other Rainbow girls will listen in and know what we are planning," remarked Red softly.

Lexie used her new ability and zoomed closer to her sister's face. Helen and the rest seemed to be in a trance. Their eyes were glazed over as though they were deadly robots awaiting a command.

"They are hypnotised by Dr Dre, so I think that their psychic abilities have been disconnected."

"There's only one way to find out," said Violet, "can you hear me?"

The three girls went into telepathy mode.

"Loud and clear," replied Lexie.

"No interference here so what's first?" asked Red.

"You girls take on your sisters and I will deal with the other eight girls," replied Lexie telepathically.

"I'm not fighting my sisters," complained Violet.

"I'm not challenging Tamir to a dual," stated Red.

"I can't take everybody on," commented Lexie in a raised tone.

"I know that you girls are conspiring to get to me," interjected Dr Dre.

"He's hoping," said Violet, "we are trying to work out how to overpower our sisters without getting our butts kicked."

"We will get to you next," was Lexie's reply to Dr Dre.

The four Rainbow girls slowly approached.

Lexie looked to her big sister Red for help.

"You are a big sister so you can definitely take on Tamir."

"Thanks," replied Red telepathically just as the four girls stood before them, looking mean and ready for a battle.

"Surrender now or suffer the consequences," warned Tamir coldly.

"You wouldn't hurt your little sisters, would you?" begged Violet.

Tamir swung hard with a right hook towards Violet, who managed to duck just in time. Then she went and hid behind Roxie Red. Tamir proceeded to punch and kick Red, who blocked a few but staggered back from the sheer power. Violet was exposed and Helen jumped in to fight, leaving Lexie battling against both Gloria and India!

"How come I get to fight two people at the same time, while you get one each?" complained Lexie telepathically.

"Do you want to swap and have Tamir?" said Red, avoiding another big right hook.

Violet struggled to hold off Helen and was hit with a spinning heel kick.

"Ooh, you little brat," yelled Violet while jumping back up to her feet.

"I don't know how long I can hold off Tamir before she knocks me out," complained Red.

"Why don't you try burning her like you did to break you out of your trance," suggested Lexie using telepathy.

Tamir showered Red with punches and caught her on the jaw. Red zapped her with her x-ray vision, but Tamir's force field protected her.

"Well that didn't work," squealed Red.

Lexie blocked both Gloria and India's strikes, then returned a few of her own. Now using 80% of her super abilities, Lexie sped up and managed to strike them both.

"Sorry sis," said Lexie who was now on the attack.

Dr Dre sat with the President and watched as the Rainbow girls battled against their sisters.

"Help," screamed Red running past Lexie with Tamir hot on her tail.

Lexie exchanged some hand techniques with Gloria before turning to defend herself from India. Then Lexie remembered that she had burnt Violet and managed to break her out of her hypnotic trance. After blocking a few more strikes, she held India's arm tightly using her Kung-Fu grip. Gloria came in for an attack, but Lexie anticipated her next move and kicked her across the room. She held India even more tightly as she struggled to break free.

India screamed in agony. Lexie had now burnt her wrists and the heat awoke her from her hypnotic trance.

"What's going on?" asked India dizzily.

"Welcome back sis," answered Lexie joyfully.

After a few seconds, India's psychic connection returned.

"Is that you India?" asked Red in telepathy mode.

"Yes."

"I really need your assistance dealing with Tamir."

India reached into her magic belt and pulled out some small wheels. She threw them in the air towards Tamir and they grew into giant rubber tyres before landing over her head. The wheels tightened their grip as Tamir struggled to break free.

"My rubber wheels won't hold her for long," advised India.

Red turned her head towards Lexie for assistance. Dr Dre stood up in frustration. Pointing his arm towards them, he said,

"Get them, destroy them all."

The other eight girls joined in and began to fight. Most of them descended upon Lexie.

"Why me?" complained Lexie now fighting Gloria and several others at the same time.

Lexie managed to hold tightly onto Gloria's arms with the hope that she would give herself a friction burn, but Phoebe approached. Lexie quickly floated off the ground and landed somewhere else in the room still holding tightly onto Gloria. Then to Lexie's surprise, Gloria used Wing-Chun to break free.

"Oh no you didn't," complained Lexie trying to grab her once more.

"Are you having trouble over there?" Red asked in telepathy mode.

"She's too skilful, maybe you should zap her with your heat vision."

"Hold her still then," ordered Red.

Lexie fought on, and eventually grabbed both Gloria's wrists. She held tightly using her Kung-Fu grip, at the same time as gradually turning her bum towards Red.

"Now," screeched Lexie.

Red stared carefully and a laser beam came out of her eyes converging onto Gloria's bum.

"Ouch!" squealed Gloria, "why did Red burn my butt?"

"Dr Dre had you in a trance and he compelled you to attack us," replied Lexie, "and I think that Red is about to need your help with restraining Tamir."

Gloria quickly floated over to assist Red who was now backing off from Tamir who had managed to break free from the rubber tyres and walking slowly towards her looking mean.

Violet was in a corner fighting Helen. Somehow, she was on her back attempting to hold on, but Helen used a Judo throw and Violet flew over her shoulders and landed hard on the ground.

"I quit," Violet joked.

"Do you need some help controlling Helen?" asked Lexie in telepathy mode.

"Err, yes," answered Violet slowly backing off from Helen.

Goldilocks approached Lexie kicking and punching. Lexie gave her a hard roundhouse kick to her head, which knocked her to the ground and gave her some time to run over and help her big sister.

"You take Goldilocks and I'll deal with Helen," ordered Lexie.

"Good luck little sis," replied Violet just as Goldilocks came in with a powerful strike.

Lexie battled with Helen who was much taller. She managed to hold onto one of her arms and with her other hand she gave Helen a hard slap to the face.

"Wake up," Lexie shouted.

Helen slapped her right back saying,

"See how you like a slap."

Lexie then sent a message to Roxie Red in telepathy mode saying,

"I think that I need help with Helen."

Several girls zoomed through the air. Lexie peered up to see Gloria and India trying to catch Tamir, who was chasing Red.

"Not much I can do from up here," responded Red frantically.

Lexie fought on, blocking kicks and punches from big sister and trying her best not to hurt her. Fending off an attack from the twins, Lexie's lightning reflexes caught Helen's arms at the same time as kicking both Rachel and Rebecca. They tumbled across the floor giving Lexie time to call out once more for Red's assistance. Both Gloria and India were now holding onto Tamir's legs, preventing her from moving. Red turned and zapped Helen in her bum, but her force field was too powerful and repelled the blast.

"It didn't work," moaned Lexie disappointingly.

"Unless you can weaken her force field, there's nothing I can do," replied Red.

Lexie's seven rainbow crystals began to flash as she attempted to channel Helen's energy from her enchanted belt. Helen's force field was now down, she sent another message to Red to try again. Red aimed towards her bum and fired once more.

"Ouch! What was that for?" complained Helen with a puzzled face.

"Welcome back big sis."

"My butt hurts," moaned Helen.

Lexie gave a warm smile and said,

"I think that they need more help over there with restraining Tamir."

"Don't you need help here little sis?"

Lexie slowly turned her head to face the twins and said,

"No, I've got this."

Helen floated off and joined the others.

The twins stood in front of Lexie and stared her down. She tried to compel them by blinking to make a psychic connection, but failed. The twins were now under Dr Dre's hypnotic spell and no longer able to control. Lexie resorted to say,

"I guess I'm just gonna have to knock you both out."

"You are outnumbered," replied Rachel, one of the twins.

Lexie glanced over to her left, right and behind her and noticed another three girls approaching. The twins made a slight move forward. Lexie's reflexes were too quick and she kicked in front, behind and then jumped in the air to perform a split kick to her left and right at the same time. All the girls were down and just Rachel stood before her.

"You were saying?" reaffirmed Lexie confidently.

Rachel moved again and was caught with a jump back kick which knocked her across the room, and she tumbled to the floor.

Another girl approached. It was Phoebe the Witch, who said, "Are you ready for round two?"

Lexie returned, "Bring it witch."

They began to fight, first blocking and then striking each other in hand-to-hand combat. Lexie was caught with an unexpected punch which knocked her down.

"Eat dust," bellowed Phoebe.

"Eat this," replied Lexie jumping to her feet and striking her to the head with a roundhouse kick.

Phoebe staggered back, reached into her pocket and threw some green dust into the air. It slowly came back down and reassembled itself as another witch dressed in green.

"Meet my sister Elsa."

Lexie paused to observe her opponents, who looked identical apart from Elsa having long green hair. Before she could attack, the other four girls surrounded her once again.

"You're evil," said Lexie.

"I'm evil, but my sister is... wicked," replied Phoebe.

Elsa also spoke and said, "Now, let's crush the little bug."

The girls attacked and began to knock Lexie around. She struggled for a few more seconds until she finally connected Elsa with a hard hook punch to her jaw. Then she said, "Now try 90% of my abilities."

Lexie sped up, first blocking and then striking each girl in turn. She jumped and kicked, blocked, and countered, but Kiera caught her with a powerful sidekick. She staggered backwards and for a split second wished that she had more than one of her to fight them. The amber crystal on her magical belt flashed a few times and the six girls spun their heads around in confusion. There now stood five more copies of Lexie. She had now discovered that she had the power of Astro projection and could conjure copies of herself.

For a moment the girls stood not sure which one to attack. Then Lexie, along with her copies jumped, spun and somersaulted around. The six girls began to punch and strike, but all except one connected. The other images of Lexie were holograms. Lexie continued to confuse them by quickly swapping places with her holograms and lashing out at her opponents before they could discover that they were fighting against the wrong one. Now, on the floor lay six girls moaning and groaning in pain, before Roxie Red walked over and said, "Do you need any help?"

Lexie laughed and said, "Yeah sure, you can take over now."

Red glanced around to see several girls groaning on the floor surrounded by several images of Lexie.

"Did Tamir hit me so hard that I have double vision, or can I see several copies of you?"

"I have just discovered a new ability of Astro projection," replied Lexie cheerfully.

They turned their heads to look over their shoulders to see Violet struggling to finish off Goldilocks, Dominoah and Asha-D.

"I'll go and help Violet and you go and see if you can restrain Tamir."

Lexie agreed with Red and headed over to assist Gloria and India, who were still holding onto Tamir's legs, while Helen held her in a tight bear hug from the back.

"You girls need help?" asked Lexie sarcastically.

"I can't hold her for much longer," moaned Helen.

"You girls release your hold, I'll take it from here," said Lexie confidently.

They all released their grip and Tamir quickly jumped to her feet. Lexie then walked over to Tamir and slapped her in the face, but she didn't even flinch.

"Was that supposed to hurt?"

Lexie then slowly stroked Tamir's face nervously and said,

"Sorry big sis, but this is gonna burn."

Tamir quickly gave Lexie a barrage of punches, but her reflexes were too quick, she dodged out of the way. Lexie was using 90% of her speed and Tamir's punches almost appeared to travel in slow motion. Tamir came back in with some big swings towards Lexie's jaw. This time Lexie quickly blocked and held tightly onto both her wrists. Tamir struggled to break free, but Lexie held on firmly with her Kung-Fu grip. Dr Dre watched as his last hope was overpowered by this little girl with amazing super abilities. Lexie's Golden leather belt and the seven rainbow crystals flashed rapidly as she began to drain the energy from Tamir's enchanted belt and temporarily shut down her force field. Then she called to Roxie Red in telepathy mode, who gave Asha-D a last hook punch before turning to face Tamir. She fired and Tamir yelled out, "Who has just burnt my butt?"

Lexie along with Helen, Gloria and India began to laugh loudly.

"Welcome back big sis," replied Lexie.

Tamir turned to face Dr Dre, who was looking furious and in a commanding tone yelled,

"Rainbow girls."

They all had their psychic connection restored and understood the command, stood up, reached into their leather belts and pulled out their chosen weapons. Tamir had her golden gloves, Gloria produced a miniature stick, which magically grew into a long wooden staff, India pulled out of her white leather belt a handful of small blue wheels, which when thrown into the air would magically grow into giant rubber tyres that tightened around their victims. Roxie Red pulled out a short spear, Helen produced a handful of white darts shaped like stars, Violet pulled out two short escrima sticks and Lexie chose to use just one set of Nunchucks. Then the Rainbow girls confidently stood awaiting their opponents.

The eight girls along with Phoebe's sister Elsa, the wicked Witch of the west, slowly approached. For a moment they all stared directly into each other's eyes, with only seconds away from the final showdown. The Rainbow girls lined up in their different colours, which represented each colour of the rainbow. Roxie Red was first, then Lexie in amber, Gloria in yellow, Tamir in green, Helen in blue, India represented indigo and Violet was on the end.

Chapter 17

There was a mass of screams before they all began lunging towards each other. Asha-D attacked Tamir with her long legs, trying her best to stay away from her hands. Tamir showered her with punches, but Asha-D used her Olympic Taekwondo to manoeuvre out of the way. Gloria and Jet exchanged techniques blocking and countering each other. Jet used her traditional Karate and Gloria Wing-Chun Kung Fu. Kiera attacked India, who was able to easily overpower her with just one arm before throwing some small blue wheels into the air. They then came back down and descended upon her. The wheels tightened and Kiera was trapped.

Dominoah chose to attack Helen who battled for a short while before connecting with a slipping sidekick. Dominoah then ran in with a rugby tackle, but Helen jumped high out of the way, causing Dominoah to collide with a wall. Helen then took advantage and threw a few darts into her bum. There were screams of pain. Roxie Red took on Rachel and Rebecca the twins, but her fight was cut short as Violet approached her in desperation.

"What's wrong little sis?" asked Red.

"I was fighting Goldilocks," replied Violet sounding slightly out of breath, "and then three small replicators appeared by her feet."

"What's so scary about that?" asked Red, kicking the twins across the room with ease.

"They then grew into them," screamed Violet pointing behind her.

Red turned her head to look over her shoulder. Standing in the distance was Goldilocks and… three bears!

Goldilocks smiled triumphantly back towards them.

"I guess it's time for the big bad wolf to get a bite to eat," said Red, now pulling her red hood over her head.

Red's metamorphosis slowly changed her into a wolf as she ran over towards Goldilocks. The three bears attacked her, but the wolf was bigger than the little bear and easily bit his bum. He screamed in pain. Then it was time for mamma bear. Red ran circles around her until she had a clear view of her rear, then she gave her bum an almighty bite. Just big bear left, who was taller than the wolf, but not as fast. Red's quick reflexes were still present as a wolf and she dodged out of the way of a few strikes. Then she stood up on her hind legs and pushed him over with her front paws, turned him over and bit him hard in his bum. Goldilocks stood alone, not sure what to do, I mean, who would want to attack a big bad wolf! Red approached her and stared into her eyes. The wolf howled loudly, as Goldilocks began to say,

"My, what big eyes you have."

In a deep voice, the wolf said,

"All the better to see you."

"My, what a big nose you have."

"All the better to smell you."

"And my, what big teeth you have."

"All the better to eat you."

The wolf lunged forwards and took a bite of her butt. Goldilocks screamed in pain and then quickly vanished out of sight.

The wolf then casually trotted back over to Violet, while slowly transforming back into the beautiful Roxie Red.

Violet battled against the twins using her escrima sticks. In the end she just hit them both across the head with her sticks and knocked them both out.

"Down and out," said Violet, sounding quite proud of herself.

"You what!" said Red, "I finished three bears faster than you."

They chuckled together and then turned their heads to watch the others. Lexie was having some trouble with the two witches. Elsa kept building a wall of ice between them, preventing her from finishing her off. Phoebe kept flying around on her magic broomstick and firing beams of light that knocked Lexie off balance. Her force field withstood the blows, she was soon back in for more. She spun her Nunchucks around her body and performed an Arial display, before striking, but the ice was too tough and stood firm. Lexie shrank her Nunchucks and placed it back into her belt. Then she glided high into the air before swooping back down to perform a Karate chop. This time the ice cracked and broke in two. Phoebe prepared to strike once more, but then out of nowhere came several rubber wheels flying through the air. They slowly grew, tightened around her as they descended down and rendered her out of action. Lexie then gave Elsa a last spinning heel kick to the head. She fell to the ground and remained unconscious.

The Rainbow girls turned their heads to observe Gloria battling against Jet, who now had a samurai sword in her hand. She swung violently towards Gloria who was using her wooden staff. Gloria's reflex was too quick. She blocked the samurai sword and connected with her fingers. This forced Jet to release her grip and the sword fell to the ground. Out of nowhere, several more wheels flew through the air and swooped down. They tightened around Jet's torso and rendered her out of action. Gloria joined the other Rainbow girls, who had all now turned to face Dr Dre.

"Give up, you are outnumbered," said Lexie.

He glanced around the room to see his fleet of fighters unable to continue. Helen had used strands of her magically enchanted hair to bind Dominoah's wrists and ankles, Tamir had finally knocked Asha-D out using her golden boxing gloves and most of the others were trapped within several layers of rubber tyres from India. Wiping a hand across his mouth Dr Dre said,

"Never."

He reached into an inside pocket of his jacket and pulled out a pair of gloves. They were padded and one seemed unusually large.

"Gonna try and do your dirty work yourself?" asked Lexie.

He slowly put them on and said,

"I guess I'll have to finish you all off myself."

The Rainbow girls chuckled.

"I'll get him back for what he did to my parents," said Violet.

"No, let me at him. I'm hungry and need another bite to eat," expressed Red.

"Let me throw a few darts into his butt," added Helen.

Lexie stood back and observed Dr Dre who appeared slightly too confident.

"No, I want to kick his butt," insisted Violet.

"We will play rock, paper, scissors," suggested Red.

The three girls began to play rock, paper, scissors, until Dr Dre interrupted them saying,

"I'll take all three of you at the same time."

"This should be easy," said Helen, "I'm gonna make you pay for poisoning me."

She approached and threw a few white darts which pierced deep beneath his skin. He screamed in agony at the same time as removing the darts and then throwing them to the ground.

In just a few seconds, his skin regenerated, and he smirked back towards her saying, "I'm immortal and can regenerate from any injury I sustain."

"Eat this," yelled Helen whilst performing a powerful roundhouse kick to his face.

He staggered and then raised his right hand just as she tried to finish him off with a punch. There was the sound of static heard, before Helen flew backwards and fell to the ground. The Rainbow girls glanced down towards Helen in sheer surprise of what had just happened.

Violet glided towards him and began to fight, blocking and countering his techniques. Then out of nowhere came the sound of static once again and Violet too flew back. Lexie used her new power and zoomed in closer. There she could see a slight bulge in his right hand. Roxie Red floated towards him and fought hard, while Lexie swiftly ran over to Violet saying,

"He's got something in his right hand, under his gloves. Can you try and see beneath the surface?"

Violet used her thermal imaging ability and discovered something horrifying.

"He's got the other part of the crystal."

"It must be giving us an EMP blast which is causing the sound of static," exclaimed Lexie.

Just then, Roxie Red flew across the room and tumbled to the floor groaning in pain.

"We are in trouble," said Violet, "it's penetrating our force field."

"Warn the others using your telekinesis," ordered Lexie, "I'm gonna take the President to the church for safety."

Lexie glided over to the President, who was now sitting alone behind his desk. He turned to Lexie and said,

"Leave young lady before you get hurt."

"I'm not leaving without you Mr President. I am taking you somewhere else for safety."

Lexie grabbed his hand. Before he could shrug her off, they vanished and re-emerged in a church. A priest approached and asked them if they were okay. Lexie then said,

"Please could you anoint the President with your Holy oil, because I think that he is hypnotised and under some evil spell."

The Priest rubbed some oil onto the side of the President's head and wet the mark. Within seconds the President awoke from his hypnotic trance and was no longer compelled to do Dr Dre's bidding.

"You are now blessed," said the Priest.

"What happened, why am I here?" asked the President.

"You were brainwashed by an evil villain, so I transported you here for safety and now I'm going to go and deal with the homicidal maniac for you," replied Lexie.

"But you are just a little girl."

"I have special abilities Sir."

"Then go save the world and may God be with you."

In a flash, Lexie vanished.

She teleported back into the large room where her sisters were still battling against Dr Dre. Tamir had just punched him in the face, first with a right and then with a big left hook. His jaws sunk in as though she had crushed his skull, but before Lexie's very eyes, she saw his body quickly regenerating. All his injuries had disappeared, he was now back up fighting against the other girls. One by one they first connected him with a technique and then there was the sound of static before they flew across the floor in agony. Lexie quickly ran over to her big sister Tamir and knelt down to assist her back to her feet.

"It feels like he is using a Police Taser on us."

"Then how will we ever defeat him?"

"I don't know little sis, but you better come up with a good idea soon."

Lexie watched as her Rainbow sisters fought on courageously. They kicked and punched before somersaulting out of the way of another EMP blast. They surrounded Dr Dre and attacked him from all directions. He sounded so tired that he could hardly catch a breath. Red caught him with another laser blast from her eyes which penetrated through his force field and fried his skin, but they watched him heal rapidly. Lexie then sent out a message using telekinesis saying,

"Let's combine our forces and attack him at the same time. Our abilities are far greater combined together."

"Unity is strength, so all together girls," commanded Tamir.

Their psychic connection was made and all the Rainbow girls lined up in their order of the rainbow, Red first and ending with Violet standing on the end of the line.

Dr Dre stood resolute and full of confidence in his alien crystal. Roxie Red gave the signal, they all flew towards him at a speed that caused the colours of the rainbow to be seen. They all connected with Dr Dre at the same time and knocked him flying through the air and tumbling to the floor. He scrambled to his feet just as they hit him once more. Badly bruised he slowly got back up. The rainbow of colours hit him again almost destroying his body, but each time his cells regenerated at an alarming rate.

"I have absolute power," he screamed at the top of his voice.

"We need to end him," bellowed Violet.

"We need to find the secret to his powers," said Red.

"His powers reside in his belt," advised Lexie.

"Then let's take it off so Lexie can overpower him," said Violet.

"Why me?" questioned Lexie.

"What powers are you packing these days?" asked Tamir.

"She can project several hologram images of herself," exclaimed Violet.

"That's it," said Lexie, "you all attack him at the same time, while I confuse him so that he doesn't realise I am trying to unfasten his belt from around his waist."

Just then a voice came from Dr Dre saying,

"You'll never destroy me, give it up."

"I was told never to give up," stated Lexie.

"You can't change the course of history, this is my world," insisted Dr Dre.

Roxie gave her order using her psychic connection and they all flew towards him creating another rainbow of colours, while Lexie conjured several holograms of herself. She surrounded him, while the others launched strikes on his body. Then Lexie hit him. He got up and became confused with the six images of Lexie that were now approaching to make their move. She punched and he blocked and then gave her an unsuccessful right hook that passed straight through her.

"That's not possible, how did you do that?" he asked indignantly.

Lexie kicked from his left and he fell to the ground. Dr Dre became angry and frustrated, no longer knowing which image to trust as the real one. The Rainbow girls hit him. Holograms of Lexie approached from all directions, he unsuccessfully swung from left to right. The real Lexie was behind him and at lightning speed, managed to unfasten his belt, then vanished in a flash and reappeared between Roxie Red and Gloria.

The seven Rainbow girls stood before him. He gazed towards Lexie's hand and saw his magic belt dangling in defeat. His trail of thought stopped abruptly as his eyes widened.

"You're finished. This contemptible act of evil cannot go without punishment," said Lexie.

"You're scared to admit that we want the same thing, to build a better World," replied Dr Dre.

"Do you call this better? Where is everyone?" asked Lexie.

"This is my world and people will follow my commands or perish."

"You have performed mass executions, mutilation and who knows what else, just to get your own way?" bellowed Lexie in a raised tone.

He kept shaking his head in disagreement saying,

"No, I have created peace."

"You have caused the end of the world," said Red.

"He is a homicidal maniac," added Violet.

There was a short moment while they stared towards each other.

"Your power resides in this belt, so without it, we will finally defeat you," said Lexie.

"Now can I bite his butt?" asked Roxie Red.

"Go get him Little Red Riding Hood," replied Lexie.

Red pulled the hood of her red cloak over her head and smiled. Then she walked forwards and slowly transformed back into the big bad wolf. Dr Dre's eyes widened once again as the wolf growled. It jumped up and began to attack him, scratching him with her paws and then taking chunks out of his flesh. He tried to fight back but was unable to overpower the wolf. Dr Dre turned away in fear and Red had a clear path to his bum. The wolf bit his butt and Dr Dre screamed in agony.

"I beg you for mercy."

"You sound like a pathetic fool," bellowed Lexie just as Red took another bite of his butt.

In desperation, he pulled off his right glove and revealed the Alien crystal in the palm of his hand. Red sensed danger and quickly flew into the air. The wolf then slowly transformed back into Roxie Red as she slowly glided down to the ground and joined the other Rainbow girls. She then lowered her hood of her red cloak and said, "That crystal possesses immense power."

"We need to really take him out," said Lexie.

"How?" asked Violet.

"Attack him with everything you've got."

There was a wave of rainbow colours that headed towards him. At lightning speed, they all used their special abilities to try and destroy him. Helen swung her head from left to right and several magical strands of her blonde hair flew into the air. They circled around Dr Dre in search of an opening, but couldn't penetrate his force field which was now powered by the crystal. India threw several blue wheels that swooped down over him. They slowly squeezed, but failed to tighten hard enough. They then recoiled and returned back into India's belt. Tamir, Gloria, Violet and Lexie punched and kicked at Dr Dre's force field. Each time they felt as though they were being electrocuted. Red zapped him with lasers from her eyes and sparks were seen.

After the dust settled, Dr Dre stood with a crooked smile on his face saying, "The fate of the world now lies in the palm of my hand."

Chapter 18

The Rainbow girls looked to their little sister Lexie the Oracle, for guidance. Lexie stared towards Dr Dre with a fixed gaze, while her mind tried to process a tangled web of thoughts.

"He has that Alien artefact, and its powers are self-sustaining."

"It must have a weakness," whispered Violet.

"The crystal might not, but every man has a weakness," replied Lexie telepathically.

"Even if he is supposed to be immortal?" asked Violet.

"We can't get near him without being electrocuted from the EMP pulse," advised Tamir.

"You can't, but I can," said Lexie.

"How?" asked Violet.

"I can use your powers to amplify mine."

"To do what?" asked Tamir.

"I will absorb all the power from the crystal and then direct it into Dr Dre and give him an overload similar to a lightbulb being powered by a Nuclear reactor."

"And what of you?" asked Violet.

The Rainbow girls turned their faces towards Lexie as she said,

"I was brought here to save the world."

"That sounds too risky," interjected Roxie Red.

"It has to be me."

With that, Lexie slowly walked forwards.

There was tension in the room. Lexie now stood before Dr Dre and they stared into each other's eyes. A few seconds past before Dr Dre said, "You declared war, well now Vengeance is mine."

Lexie replied saying, "Enough games, let's end this."

Dr Dre extended his right arm, containing the Alien crystal. "Put this in your palm and allow me to control you and finally have your powers, or I will finish off your Rainbow sisters."

Lexie received some messages in telepathy mode.

"Please don't touch it little sis," advised Red.

"Let's forget today and fight him tomorrow," said Violet.

"There's no other way," replied Lexie calmly.

Her golden belt began to illuminate. Then her amber crystal flashed a few times, as it tried to connect with the other Rainbow girls magical belts. Finally, all seven rainbow crystals on Lexie's belt glowed brightly. Her power increased exponentially, while she channelled their energy.

"Nothing in this world can harm me," cackled Dr Dre nastily.

"Lucky I'm not from your world," said Lexie.

She extended her arm as though she was going to take the crystal, but then held onto his hand so that they were connected. The crystal sent out an EMP pulse that electrocuted her. Lexie stood there and absorbed the energy.

"What are you doing?" asked Dr Dre shakily while trying his hardest to release from her hold.

Lexie's Kung-Fu grip held him tightly as he began to panic. She started to shake violently as more energy flowed through her body from the crystal. The Rainbow girls experience a weird sensation, while Lexie uses their powers to amplify hers. All their belts around their waists were now flashing brightly.

"What's she doing?" asked Roxie Red.

"She's draining the crystal," commented Tamir.

"No," exclaimed Violet, "she's saving the world."

When Lexie sensed that she had absorbed enough energy from the crystal, she looked at Dr Dre with a fixed gaze saying, "Now we will finally defeat you."

Lexie transferred all the stored-up energy from the crystal and directed it through her right arm and into Dr Dre. He screamed violently as more energy flowed through his hand, which was securely fastened to Lexie's. His powers increased exponentially, they both shook from the Taser effect. A rainbow travelled from the girls and into Lexi. She absorbed and released the kinetic energy through her arm, into his.

"Let me go," screamed Dr Dre, now begging for mercy.

"Eat this," replied Lexie.

She focused on holding him tightly until he received an overload of energy. Lexie's Kung-Fu grip was too strong, and Dr Dre failed to break free from her hold. For a few seconds they both shook violently from being electrocuted. They both then fell to the ground with an almighty thud.

Red held her hand firmly against her mouth to prevent herself from screaming, while Violet quickly floated over, crouched down and held Lexie in her arms. Gloria was first to arrive and proceeded to take her pulse.

"Well?" asked Violet nervously.

"She's gone."

"Violet screamed,

"NO!"

Helen came over and took Dr Dre's pulse, then said,

"He's dead."

"She sacrificed herself to save everybody," said Tamir.

"What an honest and unselfish act of kindness," added India.

The psychic connection with Lexie was severed and nobody could sense her anymore. They all looked down at the two motionless bodies. Helen glanced around in search of the Alien crystal but was unable to find it.

"The crystal has disappeared."

"Who cares," said Red, "at least he's finally Defeated."

"She was so Courageous," said Violet softly, whilst slowly stroking Lexie's face compassionately.

They all glanced down at their little sister, lying there with her long black hair tied up in a high ponytail, just as she always liked it and her pale white face with her eyes closed, looking at peace. With the world.

"She's gone," said Red, "it's time to let her go."

Roxie Red approached and held out her arms to take Lexie. Then suddenly Violet sprung to her feet, still with Lexie in her arms and bellowed, "No, no, no, I refuse to let her go."

Then Violet vanished. The other Rainbow girls turned their heads to look towards each other, not knowing what to do.

"Should we go after her?" Red asked.

"No, let her go and have time to grieve," replied Tamir.

Chapter 19

The bell sounded to signify the end of school. Students rushed out, headed down the corridors to retrieve their coats and head to meet at their planned destination.

"Come on, hurry up," ordered Helen, "I want to get a good seat."

"I can't find my coat," replied Nadia.

"Here it is dear," said a boy's voice in a strong Irish accent.

Nadia turned around to see Seamus holding her coat and smiling cheerfully back towards her.

"You are so lucky you are cute," responded Nadia warmly.

"Please," said Helen, "will you two just get a room."

"You are just jealous he's my man," answered Nadia.

"Come on, let's get out of here and see our girl," returned Helen.

As Lexie slowly opened her eyes, she waited for the room to become in focus. Then she heard a faint voice say,

"Be strong, don't be afraid because you are healed."

"What?" asked Lexie, now frantically looking around the room for the owner of the voice, but there was nobody to be seen.

"Lexie, Lexie," another faint voice called.

Lexie slowly looked around as the scene before her slowly became more focussed.

"Where am I?" asked Lexie in a slurred tone.

"You are in the hospital, I am Doctor Draper."

"What, what happened?" asked Lexie in a more confused tone.

"You've just awoken from a coma."

"Where are my parents?" asked Lexie shakily.

"They are just outside the door; I will call them in and let them know that you are awake."

The Doctor left the room and seconds later Lexie's parents entered along with Doctor Draper.

She looked at her parents and then Doctor Draper in confusion.

"Am I dead?"

"No, you are very much alive," replied her parents.

"How is this possible?" Lexie asked.

"You have been in a coma for nearly a year and have suddenly woken up," answered mum.

"And it is somewhat a miracle," added Doctor Draper.

"No, no, we have done this before," Lexie expressed disappointingly.

"Done what?" the Doctor asked.

"You call me a miracle and then let me go home, because my scars from my kidney replacement have healed rapidly."

Baffled, her parents turned their heads to the Doctor and then back to face Lexie. Her mum then said,

"You haven't had a kidney replacement."

"Then why am I in hospital?"

"You were scheduled to have a replacement, but you fell into a coma," the Doctor went on, "then you just woke up a year later and now your kidney is working fine."

"Where's the little girl that said that I was healed?"

"What little girl?" asked the Doctor.

"Violet, where is Violet?" screamed Lexie, "the girl with blond hair and big blue eyes."

"Maybe she's outside the door waiting to come in and meet you," said mum.

Lexie's mum walked over to the door and opened it.

Lexie heard shuffling outside the door that was progressively getting louder as some people approached. Her heart skipped a beat, as she grew anxious. Then to her surprise, several students entered, along with her favourite teacher Mr Knott.

"Our girl is awake," said Helen.

"Nadia, Helen, what are you guys doing here?"

"Your parents asked some of your friends at school to come and surprise you," answered Nadia.

"So, I organised a surprise class trip to see you," exclaimed Mr Knott.

"Hi there," said Seamus cheerfully.

Lexie began to cry as tears flooded down her face.

"See what you have done Seamus, you have frightened her," remarked Nadia.

"No, no," sobbed Lexie, "it's great to see you all."

Some students began to giggled cheerfully.

Then more people entered the room. Lexie sat upright to get a good look at everybody.

"And who are you?" asked Lexie, staring wide eyed towards a student with red hair.

"I'm LLinos," the girl replied in a Welsh accent, "we used to play hide and seek together when we were young."

"No sorry, you just looked like Roxie Red for a second."

"Who's Roxie?" asked Nadia.

"I dreamt she was my sister with superpowers. People called her little Red riding hood and when she became angry, she could metamorphose into a wolf."

"You mean little Red riding hood was the wolf?" asked LLinos, becoming slightly baffled.

"Yes," continued Lexie, "and you two, Rachel and Rebecca were there, and Rachel was mean to me."

"I thought that we were good friends," defended Rachel.

Students giggled some more.

"Helen, you were there four hundred years into the future."

"Was I your friend?" Helen asked.

"Yes, you were one of my Rainbow sisters and you knew how to fight really good. I knew Kung-Fu and we made it our mission to save the world."

"Save the world from who?" asked Helen.

"From him."

Lexie pointed towards Doctor Draper.

"Me?" asked the Doctor, "who was I in your dream?"

"You were an evil villain called Dr Dre, who was trying to destroy the human race with your poisonous vaccine, you eventually caused the rapture and the end of the world."

"Dweeb," muttered Seamus.

Students snorted with laughter.

"Well, that's my queue to leave you all to talk some more and then your mum and dad are free to take you home."

The Doctor left the room, while Lexie's parents began to gather her things together to prepare to leave the hospital.

Lexie continued with her fantasy story saying,

"In 400 years Dr Dre causes the apocalypse and the end of the world. He corrupted all the boys and only girls were good. The world was in chaos, so me and my superhero Rainbow sisters had to save everybody."

"Wow," murmured several students who were now munching on chocolate.

"In my dream I had a magic belt that gave me superpowers and I could fly and could also move things with my mind."

"You mean like telepathy or something?" asked Helen in a confused tone.

"Yes," replied Lexie, "and I had a psychic connection with my twin sister Violet."

"And you dreamt all that while you were in a coma?" asked Nadia.

"Yes," answered Lexie, becoming tearful again, "but it was all just a dream."

Then a boy stepped from behind Seamus and said,

"Was I in your dream?"

Lexie looked up to see Francisco, a cute kid from Mexico, who eventually became her husband, that is, in her fantasy world.

"Err, yes," stuttered Lexie with embarrassment.

"Who was I?"

"A top scientist," exclaimed Lexie.

"What an active imagination you have," remarked Mr Knott.

Lexie glanced over at Seamus and watched him eating. He was munching on a chocolate which made her very hungry. Then she automatically thought, *'Chocolate.'*

Seamus's chocolate suddenly flew out of his hand and landed securely in Lexie's.

"Wait, what just happened?" asked a puzzled Seamus.

"I told you that I have special powers," replied Lexie.

Students turned their heads towards each other, baffled and not sure what to make of what just happened. Then Helen walked over to Lexie and said, "When was the last time you ate anything?"

"About a year ago."

"How have they been feeding you?" asked Nadia.

"Intravenously."

"Wow," they all murmured.

Lexie remembered students asking her the same question a year ago, when she thought that she had a kidney replacement and had Rainbow sisters.

"You must be hungry," said Helen walking over to her bedside with an apple.

She then reached into her coat pocket, produced a penknife, but clumsily dropped it. The knife fell and pierced Lexie's arm. Before the knife could hit the ground, Lexie reached out her other hand and caught it.

"Quick reflexes," admired Seamus.

"That looks like a nasty gash you have there," said Llinos running over to her aid with her nurse-like instincts.

"Someone call a Doctor!" ordered Mr Knott in an authoritative tone.

A nurse quickly entered the room and began to wipe away the blood from the wound. On taking a closer look, she struggled to locate the cut and asked, "Where did all that blood come from?"

Mr Knott and all the other students glanced down to where they saw the wound, but it had magically vanished.

"How is that possible?" the teacher asked.

Lexie now has a Dense molecular structure that is indestructible, but wasn't aware of her other special abilities. Her parents ordered the students to kindly say their goodbyes, then they took her home.

"Home sweet home," bellowed Lexie happily.

"I still can't believe they let you go home so soon after waking up from being in a coma for about a year," said mum.

"There's nothing wrong with me," responded Lexie cheerfully, "I must be a fast healer, the Doctor did call me a miracle."

Someone else entered the room.

"Welcome home little sister," said Paula.

"Thanks," replied Lexie, now looking around for a seat to sit down.

"Happy belated New year, let's hope that 2021 is a better year for you."

Lexie froze for a second, remembering Paula making that mistake a year ago. Did she get it right in the first place? Did Lexie just have a vivid dream while under a prolonged coma?

Overwhelmed with thought, Lexie decided to go up and have a rest before having something to eat. She sat on her bed going over all what had happened. Then on remembering her superhero sisters, she slowly became overwhelmed with emotions.

"I suppose that I should be grateful to just be alive," thought Lexie.

Then she had a sudden urge to look in her little round mirror, so she rushed over and picked it up. Lexie sat there staring deeply into the mirror at her reflection, hoping to see Violet. She looked and her reflection stared back. Then she heard a horrifying cackle. It was Dr Dre's voice. She stared into the mirror and it was just her face she saw. She thought to herself that his voice was just in her head, but then Lexie heard another voice say,

"Looking for me?"

"You're just a voice in my head," muttered Lexie back to her reflection.

"I'm behind you," the voice announced.

Shivers ran down her spine. Lexie's heart began to beat rapidly as she slowly turned her head around to see… Violet standing in the doorway.

"What!" yelled Lexie in excitement, "I don't understand."

"I sensed that your psychic connection was restored, so I sent you a message using telekinesis, that you were healed."

"I thought that I was hearing things."

"No, I'm very much real."

"But the last thing I remember is being electrocuted by that Taser, so how did I get here?"

"I teleported us down the portal and back in time, to bring you to hospital. When we arrived time leaped forwards and forgot 2020," exclaimed Violet.

"The Kristal must have altered time," said Lexie.

"The universe is still trying to find a balance," responded Violet.

"Maybe the natural order of things has been restored," commented Lexie.

She ran forwards and gave Violet a huge hug.

"Nice to see you alive and well little sis," said Violet cheerfully.

"Why didn't you wait with me at the hospital?"

"We went looking for clothes in your shopping mall," replied Violet.

"Why, who else is with you?" asked Lexie, becoming curious.

There was a slight warm breeze, followed by a rainbow of colours that entered the room.

"Roxie Red, India, Gloria, Helen and Tamir, you all came back through the portal too?"

"Yep," they all replied.

"Group hug," ordered Violet joyfully.

They all ran over and gave Lexie a warm, loving hug.

"Where did you all go?"

"We went to a shop called Next, which has next level clothes," said Tamir beaming with excitement.

They shook their bags, which were full of goodies and giggled joyfully.

After a few seconds, Lexie turned to them and said,

"I am happy to be alive, but the past has changed."

"Maybe this is an alternate Universe," said Red.

"Does that mean that our future is safe?" asked Lexie.

"No," replied Violet, "in our world Dr Dre destroys us with nuclear weapons in about four hundred years."

"And, in Dr Dre's world, he destroys humans with the rapture," exclaims Gloria.

"So, mankind's existence is futile," remarks Lexie, "we are destroyed in four hundred years either way, unless we learn to love one another and agree on world peace now!"

"We need to travel back in time to when it all went wrong," ordered Tamir.

"You can't change the course of history," said Lexie.

"We can try," said Helen.

"Let's go back to 1908 to the Alien landing in Siberia," said Red.

"So, are you ready for your next mission?" asked India.

"I can't teleport without my magical belt," answered Lexie.

"Look down," ordered Violet.

Lexie glanced down and there around her waist was her golden belt.

"I don't understand," said Lexie.

"Your belt is enchanted with magic, so it becomes invisible until you need it," said Violet.

Lexie smiled cheerfully.

They all lined up in their order of colour, Red first and ending with Violet on the other end. Before they left, Lexie said,

"I thought I heard Dr Dre's voice earlier."

"He's a Figment of your imagination," replied Violet.

"Forget about Dre! He's dead and locked in my basement!" added Roxie Red.

They all giggled joyfully whilst slowly levitating off the ground.

"So... are you ready to save the world?" asked Violet.

There was a beautiful double rainbow produced high in the air before all seven girls swiftly vanished out of sight.

The end

About the author

My name is Vendon Wright and I was born on the sixth of August 1966, in the hometown of Rugby football. I was registered blind at the age of twenty-eight, after a ten-year battle I learnt how to accept my disability and concentrate on my abilities. My new skills of diverting negative thoughts into positive ones led me down a new path and I taught myself how to touch type, using a talking computer. Now every morning I wake up with a purpose. I now write books in total darkness and now find myself writing books for both children and adults on how to positively handle stressful and difficult situations that they too might encounter during their lives.

During my journey I experienced a wide range of emotions as I fought to find a way to deal with stress, anxiety and depression at the same time as accepting my disability. After a long hard and emotional battle, overcoming huge obstacles, I finally learnt to embrace my medical condition.

In July 2017, after attaining a 7th Degree Black Belt, I was recognised as the first registered blind Grand Master of Olympic Taekwondo in England.

Some of the children's books were written during the stressful Corona Virus pandemic of 2020. It will always be remembered as a dark and difficult time for millions of people all around the World.

Inspired by - Tanya Grant Davis

Editor – flossie crossie.

Devoted to - In loving memory of my dear sister Alirthe Wright and brother Leroy Wright, who both passed away in January 2020

BV - #0027 - 080623 - C0 - 210/148/12 - PB - 9781915657312 - Gloss Lamination